I0642142

Robinson Thornton

St. Ambrose

His Life, Times, and Teaching

Robinson Thornton

St. Ambrose
His Life, Times, and Teaching

ISBN/EAN: 9783744685092

Printed in Europe, USA, Canada, Australia, Japan

Cover: Foto ©Raphael Reischuk / pixelio.de

More available books at **www.hansebooks.com**

The Fathers for English Readers.

St. AMBROSE:

HIS LIFE, TIMES, AND TEACHING.

BY

R. THORNTON, D.D.

VICAR OF ST. JOHN'S, NOTTING HILL,
AND LATE FELLOW OF ST. JOHN'S COLLEGE, OXFORD.

PUBLISHED UNDER THE DIRECTION OF THE TRACT
COMMITTEE.

LONDON.
SOCIETY FOR PROMOTING CHRISTIAN KNOWLEDGE,
NORTHUMBERLAND AVENUE, CHARING CROSS;
4, ROYAL EXCHANGE, AND 48, PICCADILLY.

NEW YORK: POTT, YOUNG, & CO.
1879.

WYMAN AND SONS, PRINTERS,
GREAT QUEEN STREET, LINCOLN'S INN FIELDS,
LONDON, W.C.

CONTENTS.

CHAPTER XIV.

CHAPTER XV.

CHAPTER XVI.

CHAPTER XVII.

CHAPTER XVIII.

CHAPTER XIX.

ST. AMBROSE.

CHAPTER I.

BIRTH AND INFANCY.

A.D. 340–341.

I⊤ is the year A.D. 340. Twenty-eight years have
passed since Constantine the Great saw, as he declared, in vision the symbol of the Crucified, and was
bidden to hope for victory, temporal and eternal,
through Him alone; twenty-eight years since the
tyrant Maxentius lost his power and his life at the
Milvian bridge; twenty-seven since Constantine's
second edict, dated not from Rome, but from Milan,
released the Christians from the fear of persecution,
and launched the Cross on an unimpeded career of
conquest. It is fifteen years since the memorable
time when the three hundred and eighteen at Nicæa
affirmed, in the happy word Consubstantial, the truth
of the Incarnation of the Eternal Son, very God of
very God, made very man; four since the unhappy
heresiarch Arius perished at Constantinople by a
strange and sudden death; seven since the busy
brain of another enemy of the faith, not heretic, but
scoffer, Iamblichus, of Chalcis in Syria (once the kingdom of Herod Agrippa II.), was stilled in the grave;
three since the great Emperor himself deceased,

B

and left his empire to a triad of unworthy and incapable sons ; and but a few days since Constantine,
the eldest of them, grasping at the dominions of
Constans, the youngest, was slain by his partisans—a
death so well deserved, and yet so melancholy in its
circumstances, that we doubt whether to call its inflic-
tion an act of stern justice, or a miserable fratricide.
Julius I. is Bishop of Rome ; the mitre of Constantinople is still worn by the pious Alexander, the aged
opponent of Arius.   Eusebius, the historian and
courtly confessor of Constantine the Great, is sinking
into his grave at Cæsarea in Palestine.   The great
St. Basil and his brother Gregory, afterwards named
of Nyssa, are children of eleven and nine at another
Cæsarea in Cappadocia.   At the same Cæsarea his
friend, Gregory of Nazianzus, now a youth of fifteen,
has been receiving his early education, and is now
preparing, at Eusebius's Cæsarea, for his finishing
studies at Alexandria and Athens.   St. Epiphanius,
now thirty years old, is studying and praying at his
monastery of Ad, in Palestine, and St. Ephraem the
Syrian is similarly engaged at Nisibis.   St. Cyril has
lately been ordained presbyter at Jerusalem.   The
great Athanasius, now in his forty-third year, is at
Alexandria, contending at once against calumny and
heresy, and compelled to unite the vindication of his
own moral character with his strenuous defence of the
faith.   St. Jerome is a boy of nine, eagerly preparing for
the time when he shall leave his Dalmatian home to
study in the great Roman metropolis.   Another trans-
lator of the Scriptures, Ulfilas the Goth, is now about
the same age, and is being trained, somewhere in the

farther East, for his future work. Martin the Panno-
nian, destined hereafter to hold the episcopal office
at Tours during exactly the same years as Ambrose at
Milan (374-397), is now serving in the army, a young
officer of four-and-twenty. Prince Julian, now some
nine years of age, is safe at the castle of Macellum,
near Cæsarea, with his brother Gallus, learning that
Christianity which he is ere long to reject for a philo-
sophized heathenism. Photinus, at Sirmium, is con-
cocting a heresy, to be published some three years
later, and promptly repudiated alike by Catholic and
Arian. At Carthage the Donatists have been availing
themselves of the Toleration Decree of 321 to propagate that schism which was not the least of the causes
that wrought the destruction of the Church of
North Africa. It is a remarkable time, if any time
can be termed specially remarkable in the history of
that standing miracle, the Church of Christ. Many a
living Christian remembers vividly the horrors of the
tenth persecution ; not a few literally " bear in their
bodies the marks of the Lord Jesus " ; but things are
now strangely altered. Kings and queens are becoming
nursing fathers and nursing mothers of the Church ;
the Empire no longer persecutes, but recognizes Christianity ; and the only question, a question as yet un-
settled, is, which form it shall recognize, whether the
philosophical religion that Artemon and Paul of
Samosata and Arius have embellished with their eloquence and systematized with all their intellectual
power, or the simple yet wondrous faith revealed in
Scripture, preached and witnessed by many a saint,
affirmed by the fathers of Nicæa, and earnestly con-

tended for by Athanasius, the faith of the Catholic Church, that Jesus Christ is "very God of very God."

There is a commotion in the house of Ambrosius, the Christian Prefect of the Gauls—lord lieutenant, as we should say, of France, the Netherlands, Switzerland, Spain, Portugal, and Great Britain. Whether the house is at Trèves, or Arles, or Lyons, it is impossible to gather from the records we possess. But, wherever it is, the Prefect is told that he is the father of a third child and a second son, and decides that the infant shall bear his own name, Ambrosius, "the Immortal," a poetical equivalent of Athanasius, the "Deathless."

Though the elder Ambrosius was a Christian, the child was not brought to the font. The christening, which now for many centuries has followed close upon birth, was in the fourth century more usually deferred. Infant baptism was practised, but it was the exception, not the rule. The newly-born infant was claimed from the powers of evil and dedicated to God by an office of exorcism and benediction, in which salt and the sign of the cross were employed; but the Sacrament of the new birth was postponed, not from the idea that infants are incapable of grace, or that the benefits of the Sacrament are limited to those who have attained a particular stage of intellectual development, but because Christians felt strongly that the Church's one baptism was "for the remission of sins," and habitually took what we may call an exaggerated and rather Novatian view of the heinousness of post-baptismal sin. Baptism was deferred as long as pos-

sible, in order that the catechumen might receive in
it a plenary absolution, not only from original guilt,
but also from actual sin, and might be in less
danger of staining the robe of the new-born through
the heedlessness of youth. And there was an unworthy notion, too, that an unbaptized man might
safely do much as he liked ;—" let him do what he
chooses, for he is not yet baptized " is an expression
which St. Augustine has recorded for us ;—but that,
once baptized, he was tied to a stricter life; and friends
were loth to curtail the possible pleasure of the
young, and bind them down to what was wrongly
imagined to be a round of gloomy austerities.   Pre-
cisely the same error exists among ourselves, and
withholds many a one who has received Baptism and
Confirmation from the Lord's Table ; the carelessness about transgressions before baptism, the horror
at those committed after it, are by us transferred to
pre-Eucharistic and post-Eucharistic sins. It was this
dread of committing himself to too much which no
doubt led to the delay in the Baptism of Constantine
the Great. We must remember, also, that in the
earlier days of the Church, over and above the ordinary temptations to which humanity is exposed, there
was a special danger of which we know nothing, that
of apostasy in persecution. It was natural for pious
parents to hesitate, and shrink from bringing an infant
to the laver of regeneration when it was not impossible
that they and all its Christian friends might be called
to bear witness in death to their Master's name, and
their little one be left an orphan, to be educated in a
Pagan home. Such reluctance was not right, perhaps;

it would have been best to obey the Master's command, and leave the future to Him ; but it was certainly natural, and perhaps, under the circumstances,
hardly blamable, as arising from an exalted view of
the greatness of the Sacrament, and the holiness of
the baptized.

At the period of Ambrose's birth, and possibly in
his case, there was another reason which induced, or
rather compelled, Catholic Christians to delay Baptism.
So widely had Arianism spread, and so much had it
been patronized by those in high places, that it was
not always easy, and indeed was in some places impossible, to find a bishop or presbyter who could be
relied on to administer the sacrament with the valid
formula.   The divinely revealed form of words was
too often altered so as not to clash with the sentiments of the Arians ; and the orthodox were obliged
to defer baptism, lest in accepting the ministrations
of an Arianizing bishop they should be involved in
the difficulties attending a ceremony of doubtful
validity ; lest, if the officiant chose to employ an
irregular form, they should have to choose between
leaving the catechumen possibly unbaptized after all,
and incurring the risk of sacrilegious iteration of a
sufficient sacrament.

One story of the infancy of Ambrose has been preserved. His cradle had been placed in the open
court of the Prefect's house, no doubt for the sake of
air and coolness, since the cells which, under the
name of *cubicula*, were all that even the proudest
Roman mansions possessed as bed-chambers, must
have been sadly deficient in ventilation, and unsuit-

able for nursery purposes. It was the time of year when bees are abroad—probably the spring of 341,— and a swarm entered the court, and settled upon the sleeping infant's head, crawling in and out of the mouth, as though it were the entrance to a hive. The nurse was for endeavouring to drive them away; and had she carried out her intentions the child's life would have been in deadly peril. Happily, the father and mother were close at hand, and stopped her forthwith, waiting, says Paulinus, to see what would be the termination of the marvel; or, as we, looking at the occurrence in a more matter-of-fact way, should imagine, understanding the habits of swarming bees better than their domestic did. What-ever the risk of leaving the creatures alone, the danger of disturbing them would have been far greater. After a time they quitted the cradle, and flew upwards till they were out of sight; and the Prefect, with a sigh of relief, exclaimed, " If the boy lives, he will surely turn out something great."

It was a natural exclamation enough when a son had been preserved from what appeared a consider-able peril. But the belief in omens still subsisted in Gaul, and was not confined to the heathen; indeed, we can hardly say with truth that it has yet dis-appeared from any part of the prefecture of Am-brosius, even from those islands which formed its north-western extremity; and the event was held to betoken the holy eloquence and sweet persuasiveness which should, in time to come, distinguish the un-conscious occupant of the cradle.

CHAPTER II.

YOUTH AND MANHOOD.

A.D. 341–374.

OF the boyhood of Ambrose we know nothing. We may presume that he went through the childish training so graphically described by St. Augustine in his " Confessions "—the " three R's " (*legere, scribere, et numerare*), the sing-song " one and one are two, two and two are four," the Virgil and the Greek grammar, the scoldings for saying *'omo* instead of *homo*. His father appears to have remained in his high post under Constantius, who, after the assassination of his brother Constans by the followers of Magnentius in 350, remained sole ruler of his illustrious parent's empire. Three years after this event, however, the Prefect was removed by death, and the widowed mother took her sons Satyrus (who seems to have had a second name, Uranius) and Ambrose, and her daughter Marcellina, who was about to take the vows as a member of a religious order, to reside at Rome. Only a few months later was born that saint on whose life, as we shall see hereafter, Ambrose was to have so important an influence, and through him on the whole history of the Western Church—Aurelius Augustinus, of Tagaste in Numidia, son of Patricius, a heathen, and Monica, a fervent Christian. We have one anecdote of the youth of Ambrose. He remarked that his mother and sister usually kissed the hands of the clergy, and sportively offered them his own, saying, "You ought to do the same to me"; a joke for which he was very properly reproved by his mother, but which his biographer Paulinus considers to have been a fore-shadowing of the high place in the Church he was destined to fill. This is the only record we possess of this period of his life. Where he studied, and under whom, we are alike ignorant; we only know that both he and his elder brother, Satyrus, applied themselves with great success to the study of the law, and that Ambrose was, moreover, remarkable for his proficiency in Greek. His spiritual adviser was a Roman priest named Simplician, whom he loved as a father, and who, in spite of advanced age, became his successor in the archiepiscopal dignity.

These unrecorded days of Ambrose's life were full of stirring incident and varying fortune both for Church and State. The treason, or folly, of the Cæsar Gallus in Antioch was followed by his capital punishment, or murder, at Pola, in 354. Constantius, the Arian, was succeeded in 361 by Julian, the philo-sophical pervert to heathenism; his short but brilliant tenure of power was followed by the still briefer reign of the orthodox Jovian; and the eleventh year of Ambrose's residence at Rome saw Valentinian the Great exercising the Imperial authority at Milan over the West, and his weaker brother, Valens, at Constan-tinople, beginning his struggle with Procopius for the empire of the East.

Under the firm rule of Valentinian, orthodox but

tolerant, the Western Church and people were far
happier than the East under Valens, whose feebleness
led him to persecute, while his unhappy perversion to
the Arian heresy ultimately directed that persecution
against the maintenance of the Catholic faith. Autho-
rities differ as to the date of his error; one historian
(Theodoret) tells us he was orthodox till after 374,
and was led astray by his wife; another (Socrates)
puts his Arianism earlier. But that he became Arian
there is no doubt.

And so ten years more passed away, while the
defeat or pacification of Alemanni and Burgundians
in Germany, of Picts and Scots in Britain, and of
Firmus the Moor in Africa, bore witness to the
wisdom that guided the strong hand which wielded
the sceptre of the West.

In due time Ambrose entered on the business of
an advocate, and practised in the Court of the Prætorian Prefect of Italy, an officer who, under a
military title, exercised such authority over the whole
of Italy, Rhætia, and part of Africa, as Ambrose's
father had possessed over Gaul.

The brilliant young pleader attracted the attention
of Anicius Petronius Probus, who then filled this
important post; he was soon made the Prefect's legal
adviser, and not long after, in the early part of 374,
was appointed President, or, as it was termed, Consular, of Liguria and Æmilia, with the rank of senator.
This appointment included both judicial and admini-
strative functions, and compelled him to take up his
residence in Milan, a city which was then disputing
with Rome the honour of being the civil metropolis

of Italy. Probus was a Christian, and a man of high principle. He dismissed Ambrose to his new sphere of duty with words which, before the year was ended, had become prophetic : "Go, and conduct yourself not as a judge, but as a bishop."

CHAPTER III.

THE EPISCOPATE.

A.D. 374.

THE see of Milan was then filled, and had been filled for 19 years, by Auxentius. A synod held at Milan in 355 had required Dionysius, the orthodox bishop, to subscribe an Arian creed, and on his refusal driven him into exile, together with Liberius of Rome, who made so bold a stand against heresy, and, if Arian tales be true, so disgracefully repented of his boldness. Auxentius, an adherent of Ursacius, bishop of Singidunum (Belgrade), and Valens, bishop of Mursa (Essek), the Arian leaders, was, under the patronage of Constantius, substituted for Dionysius in what was then called the metropolis of Italy.

A few months after the elevation of Ambrose to his consular office, the see of Milan was vacated by the death of this Auxentius, and the appointment of a successor became the subject of the most violent party feeling. The Arian faction strained every nerve to obtain a metropolitan who favoured their views. The emperor's inclination to the side of orthodoxy was known; the number of the adherents of the Nicene faith had been steadily increasing; and it was seen pretty clearly that if the new prelate were of that number, Arianism in Italy would receive a mortal blow.

Valentinian assembled the provincial bishops, with whom the election lay, and urged them to be careful whom they put on the metropolitan throne. " Let him be," said he, " such a man as I myself may be able to submit to, receiving the reproofs he may administer (for I am but a man, and must needs often offend) as a salutary medicine." The bishops entreated the emperor to make the selection himself; desirous, no doubt, of relieving themselves from the invidious task, and dreading the exasperation which their performance of it would infallibly produce in the party whose candidate was not the object of their choice. The emperor, however, declined to accede to their request, and dismissed them to their deliberations. " The task is too great for me," he said; " you who have received the Divine illumination will come to a better determination than I could."

The church in which the Synod met was thronged with people, and the ferment was so great that apprehensions were entertained lest it should break out into a fray. The president, Ambrose, judged it to be his duty to take measures for quelling the tumult. He entered the church, and exhorted the people to concord and tranquillity. Immediately a cry arose, begun, it is said, by a single voice like that of a child, "Ambrose is bishop !" Both parties joined in accepting the proposal. With a unanimity more remarkable than, and as vehement as, their former discord, they urged Ambrose to undertake the sacred office, seeing as they did how desirous he was of promoting unity and peace, and believing that the voice which first uttered his name had proceeded from no noisy partisan on earth, but from some benevolent angel.

The Episcopate was in those days not only an honourable distinction in itself, but recognized as such by society : still it was not one to be coveted by all ; least of all to be desired, in a worldly point of view, in exchange for a high State appointment. Much danger beset the prelate's path : much care and wisdom, and a rigid self-denial, were demanded of him. The old paganism was not yet extirpated : it had to be confronted from time to time, and men were not yet sure that Diocletian's persecution was the Church's last tribulation till the coming of Antichrist. And there was Arianism in all its forms, with its kindred errors, to be met and combated, even in high places, and on ecclesiastical and civil thrones. *Nolo episcopari* was a very real sentiment with all : the worldly man shrank from a trial which brought no riches, and the timid from inevitable peril, while the devout Christian could not but think within himself " Who is sufficient for these things ? " and dread the greatness of the task. Ambrose was reluctant to undertake it. Mixed feelings, among which a humble sense of his own deficiency was the most powerful, though perhaps a distrust of the popular voice was not altogether wanting, led him to endeavour to divert from himself the sentence pronounced in his favour. The expedients he resorted to, though quite in keeping with the spirit of his age, seem to us somewhat peculiar. Leaving the church, he proceeded forthwith to his court, and then and there made a show of giving orders for the application of the torture, hoping,

it appeared, to impress the people with an idea that
he was both unjust and cruel. But they were not to
be deceived. They knew his character. A few
months of his rule had shown what manner of man
he was. They saw that his pretended tyranny was a
feint : "Thy sin be upon us," was the cry : for where
no sin was, save the venial one of self-excusation from
a weighty burden, the people might safely undertake
to bear it. Then he tried, in a somewhat singular
way, to persuade them that his moral character was
not unblemished. This was almost an actual falsehood : but it lacked the poison of a real falsehood,
for it failed to deceive : "Thy sin be upon us," was
the cry again.

He next sought refuge in flight, but without success : he was soon found and triumphantly brought
back to Milan. All thought that there was something
more than human in the circumstances of his election.
The emperor himself joined in the common belief,
and heartily accepting the choice of the people
ordered that the President should forthwith be baptized and consecrated. The provincial bishops endorsed the action of the prince and people. Ambrose
was compelled to consent to receive the office and
dignity thus enforced upon him by the whole body
of the faithful, and that not of their own mere
motion, but, as all agreed, under the manifest guidance
of a higher power. He only stipulated that the
officiating bishop at his baptism should be a Catholic,
and not an Arian. Within a week from his reception
of the sacrament he had been duly consecrated, and
was bishop of Milan and Metropolitan (December
7, 374).

CHAPTER IV.

DIFFICULTIES AND DANGERS.

A.D. 374.

IF a general view of the difficulties of the episcopal office led Ambrose to shrink from undertaking it, the special circumstances of the times must have filled him with dismay at finding himself one of the chief pastors of the spiritual flock, entrusted with a charge which seemed to place in his hands, for good or for evil, both the earthly fortunes of a large portion of Christ's holy Catholic Church, and the welfare of the Christian faith and the Christian people. For Christians, alas! were far from being united, though not three centuries had passed since the Apostle of Love bade farewell to the world, not three and a half since the Divine Master Himself offered the One Sacrifice for sin. The spirit of Antichrist, which even in St. Paul's time wrought in the children of disobedience, had given rise to many a sad schism, and many a falling away from the faith which was once for all delivered to the saints. There were Manichæans, who professed what Socrates, the Church historian, calls a " Hellenizing Christianity," a compound of Gentilism and Gospel, mingling the teachings of prophets and evangelists with those of Zerdusht and other Eastern mystics.

They held that there were two deities, two originators of existence, an evil and a good, ever in conflict, and ever to remain so till a far-distant day of final triumph for the latter. Priscillian the Spaniard was, in his revived Gnosticism, beginning to teach somewhat similar doctrines in the farther West. The heresy of Paul of Samosata, and of the earlier Ebion, that Christ was a mere man, and nothing more, was held and taught by the followers of Photinus of Sirmium, a prelate of high abilities, who, after his deposition in 351, wrote a powerful treatise against all heresies except his own. The Arians, alike in their refusal to accept the Catholic creed as enunciated at Nicæa, were divided into at least three different schools or parties. The Semi-Arians, or Homoiousians, though they would not assert the Son to be of *one* substance with the Father, were ready to acknowledge Him to be of a substance absolutely and entirely *like to* that of the Father; not seeing that to admit a second divine being like to the First Cause was in effect a denial of the unity of God. The Acacians acknowledged a likeness of substance, but not entire nor absolute. The Anomoians, followers of Aëtius, "the godless," as he was called, and his pupil Eunomius, asserted the absolute unlikeness of the Son to the Father. The Meletian schismatics in Egypt, and the Donatists in North Africa, upheld, or were inclined to, the Arian theology. Macedonius, the Semi-Arian patriarch thrust on Constantinople for eight years from 351, had given especial prominence to the logical outcome of Arianism, by denying in set terms the Deity of the Holy Spirit; and his followers, called "Pneumato-

machi," or "opponents of the Holy Ghost," maintained the coequal Comforter to be but a creature, an
emanation, or an energy.   While these denied the
" very God of very God," Apollinarius of Laodicea
and his sect assailed the perfect humanity of our
Lord, by teaching that He had no human soul, the
place of which was supplied by the Deity, and that
His body, instead of being born like that of a man,
was sent down from heaven.   There were schisms,
too, as well as heresies.   The Donatists and Meletians
have already been mentioned.   The fanatical Euchites
or Enthusiastæ, the Jumpers and Shakers of the
fourth century, had begun to disseminate their strange
fancies, and contemptuously to partake of the Holy
Eucharist as a thing which could do neither harm nor
good.   Lucifer, Bishop of Cagliari, the brave confessor
in 355 with Liberius of Rome and Dionysius of
Milan, had, owing to some squabble with Eusebius of
Vercelli, broken off from the communion of the
Church.   His schism ultimately died out, but it was
looked upon as so serious at the time, that Satyrus,
the elder brother of Ambrose, when in Africa was extremely careful not to communicate with a Luciferian
bishop, holding orthodoxy of belief to be seriously
compromised by rending the body of Christ.   Then
the Novatians,—setting up, as the Emperor Constantine put it, a ladder by which they might ascend to
heaven by themselves,—denied communion to all
who had been guilty of post-baptismal sin; not putting
limits to God's mercy, but absolutely denying the
power of the Church to pronounce absolution in such
cases.   And then, in addition to heresy and schism,

there was, as has been already observed, what still remained of the power of the old religion, a dogged, stubborn, resisting force, ready to league itself with misbelief against the truth, and with the powers of this world against the Church. " Manasseh, Ephraim, and Ephraim, Manasseh ; and they together shall be against Judah." It was an unquiet time for a Catholic prelate. Well might St. Basil, in replying to the announcement of his consecration made, according to custom, by the new bishop of Milan, exhort him to stand firm. There was much to make him quail.

CHAPTER V.

DEATH OF VALENTINIAN I.

A.D. 374–375.

AMBROSE, while receiving the education of a lawyer and a statesman, had not confined himself to secular studies. Though only a catechumen, he had been allowed free access to the sacred writings and to the works of commentators and divines, and had freely availed himself of the permission. He was not himself satisfied with his store of Christian learning. " Hurried as I was," he says in his treatise on "Duties," written in 391, "from the seat of judgment and the head-gear of a magistrate to the priesthood, I began to teach you what I had not myself learnt. So it came about that I began to teach before I began to learn ; and I have to learn and teach at the same time, because I had not had time to learn before." Still there is little doubt that he was already well prepared with theological learning; and so immediately after his unlooked-for election and consecration he began to write and to preach. If we must understand literally the expressions which he makes use of in addressing his sister Marcellina, in the preface to his three books "Of virgins," we must conclude that his oratorical powers were not great :

for he writes of himself as "unable to speak" (*loqui nequeo*), and expresses a hope that he may be gifted with the power, "like the dumb Zacharias, and the ass of Balaam." But his expressions are probably due to an excess of humility. The practised pleader in the court of the Prætorian prefect could hardly be a man of slow speech and of a slow tongue. At all events, if not an orator, he was a writer and a deep thinker. Scarcely a single year passed from that of his consecration to that of his death without the composition and publication of some theological treatise : sometimes evidently what had been orally delivered, or the transcript of notes for *vivâ voce* lectures : sometimes apparently never delivered, nor intended for delivery, proceeding from the study rather than from the pulpit. True, St. Jerome carps at some of his productions, as not original, and spoilt in the transference. But St. Jerome is not infallible ; and there are those who think that Ambrose, in altering and adopting, has improved what he has touched, instead of appearing (to use St. Jerome's phrase) like the daw in borrowed plumes.

Nor did he preach only, but at once began, according to the Apostolic precept, to reprove, rebuke, and exhort. He boldly remonstrated with the Emperor Valentinian respecting some malpractices of the magistrates, and was answered with the respectful courtesy due to his good intentions and his sacred office. " I knew how bold you were, and with that knowledge I not only did not oppose your election, but voted in your favour. Apply now, as the divine law enjoins, proper remedies to the failings of our souls." He seems to have taken the monarch at his word; for it was mainly owing to his influence that a synod was soon after held in Illyricum, which reaffirmed the Nicene faith, and its synodical letter, together with an imperial rescript, was sent to the bishops of Asia Minor.

There was, however, a difficulty which he soon had to face, far more serious than that of lecturing a willing emperor, or of addressing the assembled Church, and drawing on the stores of a theology which he had amassed, while all the while,—strange as it seems to us,—he was disregarding the precept "Repent *and be baptized* every one of you."

The winter (November) of 375 saw the sudden death at Bregetio, on the Danube (near Presburg), of the great and orthodox emperor Valentinian; brought about, it was said, by the conduct of the envoys of the Quadi. The paroxysm of fury into which he permitted himself to fall on hearing from them what was intended for a humble apology, but which he seems to have looked upon as an audacious prevarication, caused the rupture of a large blood-vessel. Surgical aid was, with some difficulty, obtained, but to no purpose : the sufferer, after an ineffectual effort to speak, accompanied with terrible struggling, soon breathed his last. Justina, his empress and second wife—espoused, if the scandal repeated by Socrates be true, during the lifetime of his first wife Severa, the mother of Gratian,—had become a pervert to the Arian heresy, and had no friendly feeling towards the Catholic who was clearing away the traces of the evil work of Auxentius. During her husband's lifetime she concealed her sentiments, or at least forbore from expressing them ; but when the restraint of his presence was removed, and she felt sure of the support of her brother-in-law Valens, the Emperor of the East, it became apparent that the orthodox had nothing to look for from her but active and undisguised enmity. Gratian, her stepson, who had now reached the age of 17, was firmly attached to his father's faith, and was proof against her persuasions ; but she used every artifice—and for a time, we are told, with success— to poison the mind of her own son Valentinian, whose tender age at the time of his father's death (4 years) left him completely in his mother's power.

Gratian had already been raised to the rank of Augustus, and succeeded at once to the Imperial throne; but, as the soldiers at Bregetio had proclaimed his infant half-brother emperor, he consented to share the dignity ; and Gratian and Valentinian the Second became colleagues of their uncle Valens. The elder had scarcely reached his twentieth year, when that uncle's tragical death made them emperors of the East as well as of the West.

CHAPTER VI.

THEODOSIUS.

A.D. 378-380.

THE Huns, a Tartar race, had, after a defeat by an Emperor of China about a century B.C., been gradually moving westward. They had reached and crossed the Volga, defeated the Alani, a tribe of Skyths who then occupied the country of the Don Cossacks, and joining the Alan warriors with their own forces, had descended upon the Goths, who occupied the tract north of the Danube, the modern Roumania. These last, after an unsuccessful resistance, determined to place the Danube between them and their savage conquerors, and entreated permission of Valens to settle themselves in Thrace, the modern Bulgaria and Roumelia. The leave was given, but the Gothic refugees were received with indignities which set their spirits on fire; and the Romans found too late that they had introduced into their territory not a band of slaves but a host of enemies. Under Fritigern their leader, and aided by some of their old foes, the Huns and Alani, the Gothic warriors encountered the Romans, commanded by Valens in person, about twelve miles from the city of Adrianople, and routed them completely. According to one account, the emperor was killed in battle, and so mutilated that his body could not be recognized; others allege that he was carried by his attendants into a cottage, which was surrounded by the enemy and reduced to ashes with all who were in it, only one youth escaping to tell the tale. This terrible reverse, from which—though it took place in the East—some date the commencement of the fall of the Roman Empire, happened on the 9th August, 378. Ambrose saw in it a judgment on the heresy of Valens.

The Goths did not fail to push their advantage. They overran and laid waste the country towards the west, as far as the Julian Alps. Devastation was naturally followed by famine, and famine as naturally by pestilence. The Bishop of Milan, at this time, when, to use his own expression, everything was in confusion through dread of barbaric invasion, was, in addition to his grief at the reverses and sufferings of his countrymen, visited with a domestic sorrow. Immediately on his consecration he had placed all his property in the hands of his brother Satyrus, who undertook to perform those secular duties which would have been an interruption to the spiritual work of a prelate. The dishonesty of a certain Prosper, who thought that he might easily evade payment of a debt to an ecclesiastic, rendered it desirable for Satyrus to undertake a journey across the Mediterranean in order to recover a sum of money due from him. Ambrose was very loth to allow his brother to go, probably knowing his health to be delicate, and fearing the roughness of the voyage in the late part of the year. Satyrus, however, insisted upon running the risk. He reached Africa, but was shipwrecked and in great jeopardy; he transacted his business, and returned to Milan with the money. But his brother's fears had been too well founded. He had scarcely reached his home before he was taken dangerously ill, and in a few days he expired in the bishop's arms, who was himself just recovering from a sharp attack of illness, through which he had been tenderly nursed by Marcellina. Two discourses, the one perhaps pronounced, the other composed, on the occasion, testify to the tender affection which the brothers felt for one another, and the sure and certain hope entertained by the survivor of a blissful reunion, which should be clouded by no fear of separation.

Gratian was far from underrating the stupendous difficulties which environed an Emperor of East and West, and from overrating his own ability to cope with them. He was but twenty when his uncle's death left him—for his partner in the purple was a child of seven—practically the sole head of a double empire. Before six months had expired, he called to his aid the ablest of his subjects, whose talents and virtues have given a lustre to the imperial name. On the 19th January, 379, at Sirmium, now Mitrovicz, the capital of Pannonia, he bestowed—some say forced—the diadem, the purple, and the title of Augustus, on Theodosius, a Spaniard of Italica (Old Seville), the birthplace of Trajan and Hadrian; a worthy son of that great general Theodosius, whom his jealous ministers had done to death not three years before for the high crime of success in Britain and Africa. To the new emperor was assigned as his portion the dominion of Valens ; there were added to it, however, Dacia and Macedonia, then under the power of the victorious Goths, and calling piteously for a protector as well as a ruler.   The year had not ended before he had gained successes over the Goths, which Ambrose considered as both a fulfilment of Ezekiel's prophecy against Gog, and a punishment for their Arianism.   Theodosius received baptism shortly after.

Ambrose, meanwhile, was not idle, nor, alas ! at peace.   The next year to that which witnessed the elevation of Theodosius brought him into direct collision with the empress dowager.   The death of the Bishop of Sirmium had rendered it necessary for him to repair thither to take part in the consecration of a successor.   This city being the metropolis of Pannonia and Illyricum, it was of the utmost importance that its chief pastor should be free from all suspicion of heresy.   Justina, who was residing at the place, used all her influence, coupled with that of her youthful son Valentinian, to procure the election of an Arian, and to exclude the Bishop of Milan, who was recognised as the leader of the Catholics, from the churches.   So high ran party feeling, that personal violence was resorted to, and a girl of the Arian faction actually laid hands upon the prelate himself. The Catholics, however, carried their point, and their candidate Anemius was chosen and consecrated. But Justina never forgave Ambrose his victory, and kept up a continual intrigue for his removal from Milan.

CHAPTER VII.

SYNODS OF AQUILEIA AND ROME.

A.D. 380–383.

ABOUT the end of 377 or the beginning of 378, Gratian, when on the eve of going eastwards to assist Valens in his troubles, had requested Ambrose to furnish him with some written instruction on the subject of the Nicene faith, which his stepmother, his uncle, and his uncle's Gothic enemies agreed in rejecting. Ambrose replied by sending him two books " On the Faith." The emperor returned the work, and was so pleased with it, that, after the load of government had been lightened by the elevation of Theodosius, he wrote a letter with his own hand to Ambrose, begging him to send him the volume again, and also to visit him, and afford him more instruction. The teaching of Macedonius had rendered it needful that the Deity of God the Holy Ghost should be explained and proved, and Gratian was anxious to be enlightened on this point as well as on the special doctrine of the Council of Nicæa. Ambrose sent the two books " on the Faith " as requested, and subsequently added to them three more books, supplementing the two he had already produced on the coequal Deity of the eternal Son. To the emperor's letter he replied in the first—or at

least the first to which a definite date can be assigned
—which we have of a long series extending to
within a few months of his decease. The tone and
diction of the bishop's letter are peculiar, and scarcely
what we should expect from what we know of his
character. They savour more of the courtly consular
of Liguria than of the stern ascetic prelate of Milan.
He excuses himself for not immediately resorting to
the imperial presence, and asks to be permitted to
defer the writing of the desired work, promising to
set about it in process of time (we know that he had
the three books " on the Faith " in hand) ; and ends
with a flourish about glory and peace which would
sound almost like a sarcasm were it not coupled with
a benediction. The promise was fulfilled in less than
two years. Early in 381 Gratian received the three
books " on the Holy Ghost."

The results at once of this teaching and of the
election of an orthodox bishop of Sirmium were
speedily seen. Two Illyrian bishops, Palladius and
Secundianus, were known to be of the party which
declined to accept the Nicene creed ; and their new
metropolitan lost no time in bringing them to trial.
A synod of bishops, from Illyricum, Gaul, and Italy,
was summoned ; and it is worthy of remark that it
was convoked by the emperor's authority, his rescript,
addressed apparently to the *vicarius* of each of the
dioeceses, or civil departments, from which the members
of the synod came, being formally read by a deacon
at the opening of the synodical proceedings. By the
advice of Ambrose, this document states, who thought
it unnecessary to bring together a large number, the
aged and infirm bishops, and those who were not

in good circumstances, were excused from attendance. The synod met at Aquileia on the 3rd September, 381. This city appears to have been chosen in preference to Milan, not only as being more central, but because there was less fear of such a tumult there as might easily have been excited in the metropolis of northern Italy. Thirty-three bishops took their seats, three of them, the bishops of Marseilles, Orange, and Lyons, being commissioners from Gaul, and two, Felix and Numidius, from Africa : two presbyters also took part in the council. The chair was taken (to use our own familiar expression) by Valerian, bishop of Aquileia; but the proceedings were conducted almost exclusively by the bishop of Milan.

Palladius demurred to the authority of the synod, and complained of the absence of the bishops of the East, who, he thought, would have taken his part; appealing to a full council, before which he professed himself ready to plead. But Ambrose disregarded all his excuses, and simply put to him the question, " Will you, or will you not, repudiate Arius and his errors ?" To this question Palladius refused an answer. He entered, however, into a verbal contest with Ambrose, and one or two of the other bishops, in which he admitted that Christ is the Son of God, and spoke of His " divinity," but declined to admit Him to be true God, or to speak of Him as equal to the Father. His companion Secundianus tried a little skirmish, but in vain. After a sitting which lasted from early morning till 1 p.m., both were, as we might expect, condemned by a unanimous vote, together with a presbyter named Attalus, who, after signing at Nicæa, had fallen away from the faith.

The decision of the synod was announced in a short letter to the churches of Gaul, and in a longer one to the three emperors (Gratian, Valentinian, and Theodosius), in which the members of the synod thank them for convening it, and beg them to carry out its decrees. They also request that the Photinians in Sirmium may be prevented from holding meetings.

We are struck with the unqualified manner in which this letter to Valentinian (now ten years old) denounces the religion which his mother was teaching him. This synodical was followed by a second, denouncing Ursinus, the old opponent of Damasus, now Bishop of Rome; and a third, requesting that a council might be held at Alexandria to put down the Arians.

The Aquileian synod was not the only one that met in the year 381. Theodosius, immediately after his baptism in 380 by the hand of Ambrose's dear friend Ascholius,[1] bishop of Thessalonica, began to take steps to check the progress of Arianism. He banished the principal adherents of that heresy, with Demophilus, the Arian bishop of Constantinople, at their head; and with the approval of a number of bishops invited the great Gregory of Nazianzus to fill the vacant post. For some reason or other,[2] this eminent man had been first appointed by his metropolitan St. Basil to the obscure see of Sasima, and then placed in his father's almost equally obscure see of Nazianzus: his translation to the primacy of the East

[1] Or Acholius: the name is variously written.
[2] Some imagine that Basil was jealous of Gregory; but it seems that Gregory was placed at Sasima by his own desire, in order that he might be better able to help Basil against the ambitious semi-Arian, Anthimus of Tyana.

was objected to on the ground of its being contrary
to an ancient canon that a bishop should be removed
from one diocese to another. In the year 380, however, Gregory was Archbishop and Patriarch of Constantinople, though he shortly afterwards retired to
Nazianzus. In May of the year 381 Theodosius
summoned the Eastern bishops to meet at the capital,
and deal with the Arian and other Church questions ;
especially the heresy of Macedonius, the deposed
predecessor of Demophilus, who denied the personal
Deity of the Holy Ghost. This synod is reckoned
as the second of the Œcumenical Councils, its
determinations having been accepted and endorsed
by the whole Church, although the 150 prelates who
composed it belonged to the eastern portion of the
empire.

A large assembly of western bishops met at Rome
in the next year (382) in a synod, which was attended,
among others, by the celebrated St. Jerome, and
formally proposed that a council should be held at
Rome. This scheme had already been pressed, in a
less formal way, on Theodosius in two letters from
the Italian bishops ; and it appears that Ambrose was
the leading spirit among them. In the earlier of the
two documents the Italians show themselves to be
labouring under a strange misconception of the state
of Church politics at Constantinople. They are ready
to give up Gregory Nazianzen, and incline to take the
part of Maximus, the Apollinarian heretic, against the
orthodox Nectarius, who had been chosen to fill the
high post from which the gentle and peace-loving
Gregory had determined to retire. They fancy the
consecration of Nectarius to have been irregular. As

he was elected and consecrated much in the same manner as Ambrose himself, being chosen by the popular voice while holding the office of prætor, the Western bishops could not with any fairness complain. In their second letter they still ask for the Council, but apologise for their errors.

The prelates of Constantinople replied to the proposal by a synodical letter, showing the great difficulty of carrying out the scheme; and called upon their brethren in the West to acquiesce in their statement of the Christian faith, and especially of the doctrine of the Holy Trinity as enunciated at Nicæa. The epistle is addressed "To the noble lords and pious brethren and fellow-ministers, Damasus, Ambrose, Brito, Valerian, Ascholius, Anemius, Basil, and the other holy bishops assembled in the great city of Rome." The name of the bishop of Milan, we see, stands second in the list, next after that of the bishop of Rome.

During this stay in the city where his youth had been spent, Ambrose had not only the great pleasure of meeting his friend Ascholius, and of visiting his sister Marcellina, but also the satisfaction of witnessing the removal of one of the last relics of paganism.

The altar of victory which used to stand in the Senate-house had been, some thirty years before, removed by the order of the Emperor Constantius, who, though persuaded to take the part of the Arians, had no fondness for heathenism; Theodoret, indeed, thinks that he was a Catholic at heart. Julian had, naturally enough, ordered it to be replaced, and there it had remained till this year (382), when Gratian, who, we may remember, was under the guidance,

D

sought by himself, of the Bishop of Milan, commanded that it should be taken away. The non-Christian or neutral senators, we understand, disapproved of this, as we might expect ; but we gather from a letter of Ambrose to Valentinian in the next year that a petition for its removal had been drawn up by the Christian senators, sent to Damasus, Bishop of Rome, and by him entrusted to Ambrose, probably as being most in communication with the imperial court.

This was the last work that the pious emperor was permitted to do for Christianity. His zeal for the orthodox faith had brought upon him the hatred of those who still adhered to the paganism of Augustus, Diocletian, and Julian, and of the half-Christian followers of Arius and his disciples. We almost seem to trace in the accusations brought against him the secret influence of Justina, who hated her stepson with a stepmother's hatred, and Ambrose, his trusted adviser, as one by whom her intrigues at Sirmium had been foiled, and whose retention of the episcopal throne at Milan was a continued and unpleasing proof of her own weakness, and the popularity of himself and his faith.

Gratian's youthful spirits (he was not five-and-twenty) led him to indulge freely, perhaps too freely, in the pleasures of the chase. He was interested in the strange customs and dress of the Alani, whom the Gothic victory at Adrianople in 378 had brought under his observation. With the heedlessness of youth, he took a body of these barbarians into his service as yeomen of the guard, and was unwise enough to appear from time to time arrayed for sport in the Skythic hunting-dress. These errors in judgment, or failures in good taste, venial in a private nobleman, were exaggerated into criminality in an emperor. And Gratian was too mild and gentle to hold firmly the government of an empire composed of discordant elements, and ready to fall to pieces from its own un- wieldiness. Discontent, once suggested, flew rapidly from west to farther west ; and the soldiery of Britain and Gaul were soon roused to revolt. They were headed by Maximus, a Spaniard, a disappointed rival of his countryman Theodosius. He was in command in Britain ; but to rule in our islands was not then the glorious office which God's providence and fifteen centuries have since made it, and he longed for a higher title and wider power. With little diffi- culty he induced his soldiers to compel him to as- sume the imperial purple, and forthwith invaded Gaul. Gratian went to meet him ; but, deserted by his troops, fled to Lyons, where he was led to believe that he would find himself in safety. The promises he relied on were untrustworthy. Andragathias, one of the officers of Maximus, gained access to him by an unworthy stratagem. Enclosing himself in a car- riage drawn by mules, such as ladies were accustomed to travel in, and giving out that it contained the wife of the Emperor, he met Gratian just as he was about to cross the Rhone and enter the city. The guards were deceived, and permitted him to approach, an opportunity of which he instantly availed himself by putting the Emperor to death : the victim in his last moments called on his beloved Ambrose. This tragic event happened on the 25th August, 383. One feels almost glad to know that the assassin perished by his own act about five years after.

CHAPTER VIII.

AUGUSTINE.

A.D. 383–385.

THEODOSIUS had only just succeeded (October, 382) in reversing the result of the terrible battle of Adrianople. He had brought the Goths to terms, but the Eastern Empire was as yet in no condition to take vengeance on a successful rebel in the West. He preferred to temporize.

The empress-mother was compelled at this conjuncture to lay aside her open enmity to Ambrose. Much as Justina detested the Bishop of Milan, it was to him that she was compelled to entrust the delicate duty of meeting and making terms with the conqueror. His diplomacy was at once dignified and successful; and it was arranged, with the consent of Theodosius, that Maximus should confine himself to the farther side of the Alps, taking Trèves for his capital, and that Valentinian should retain Italy, Africa, and Illyricum. Maximus at first rather demurred to these conditions, and demanded that the boy-emperor and his mother should at once repair to his court; but Ambrose was firm in refusing to accede to this proposal; he remained in Gaul till a messenger had been sent to Milan and returned with a decided negative, and

Maximus felt himself compelled to give way. The body of the murdered emperor, however, remained in the possession of the conqueror, who was unwilling to allow it to be conveyed to Italy, lest the soldiery should be exasperated at the sight; and the bishop was unable to persuade him to surrender it to his relatives.

Not many months were permitted to elapse after the death of Gratian before an attempt was made to induce his brother to reverse the decision respecting the altar of victory in the Senate-house. Ambrose wrote at once most strongly to the emperor, entreating him not to think of doing such an indignity to the memory of his father and brother, and to God. The matter was formally brought forward in a document presented by Symmachus, the Prefect of Rome, to Valentinian, Theodosius, and his son Arcadius, who had been already associated with his father in the Eastern empire. It sounds strangely, this last dying groan of imperial heathendom; and the very fact of its being addressed in the first instance to Valentinian, who was known to be under his mother's influence, leads us to surmise that the antagonism between the half-Christianity of the Arians and the refined paganism of Julian was felt to be far from hopeless. That Jesus must be all, or is nothing, is a truth which we read in almost every page of the Church's history, as it may be recognized in almost every moment of our spiritual life. Symmachus pleads, with a show of reason, that Valentinian I., a fervent Christian, left the old arrangement untouched, and that Valentinian II. might fairly follow his example. But even an

Arian would scarcely be moved by his argument that the famine which had lately visited Italy was a punishment for the sacrilege of disendowing the vestal virgins. The paper was forwarded to Ambrose, who sent a crushing rejoinder. He addressed himself to Valentinian only, who was still unbaptized, and under Arian teaching ; he was quite sure of Theodosius, the spiritual child of his saintly friend Ascholius. Symmachus had written much concerning the protection afforded to Rome by her tutelary gods, the dignity and purity of her priests and virgins. Ambrose shows that the old gods of Rome more often than not failed to defend their worshippers ; contrasts the Christian priests and virgins with the vestals and sacrificuli of the pagan system ; reminds the emperor that the famine in south Italy could scarcely be considered a proof of Divine wrath, since in the same year north Italy had a fair harvest, Rhætia, Pannonia, and Gaul one considerably above the average ; and ends with an *argumentum ad verecundiam*, which retorts a similar argument used by Symmachus : " If those Christian emperors are commended who refrained from altering the arrangements of their *pagan* predecessors, much more will you be commendable if you decline to reverse the decision of your *Christian* predecessor." It need scarcely be said that the plaint of the pagan party was uttered in vain.

The calling forth of Ambrose's address to the emperor was not the only advantage done by Symmachus to the Church unwittingly. In this same year (384) the Milanese being in want of a public teacher of rhetoric, applied to Rome, with a request that one might be sent them. The Prefect selected a man of some thirty years of age, an African by birth, but of high abilities, who had been teaching in Rome with great success. He was not exactly a pagan, but he was a Manichæan, which was, in the Prefect's view, nearly as good. He gladly accepted the appointment, the more so as he hoped to make the acquaintance of Ambrose, whose rhetorical powers—though the possessor himself made light of them—had a wide reputation. His name was Aurelius Augustinus. The providence of God has brought it about, through his meeting with Ambrose, that he is known to us as Saint Augustine. The bishop received his visitor courteously, and seems to have fascinated him at once. Far superior to Faustus, the great Manichæan preacher, he supplied the doubter with what he had been yearning after. While the philosopher had nothing but a vain and unsatisfying deceit to offer to that hungering soul, the man of God strengthened and refreshed it with the truth as it is in Jesus. " Read Isaiah, the evangelical prophet," was his advice to the neophyte.; " study his words carefully, but remember that the letter killeth, the spirit giveth life. The things of God must be spiritually discerned."

Soon Ambrose was visited by the mother of his Manichæan scholar, the saintly Monica. She was now to see the son of so many tears (as a worthy bishop many years before had termed him) brought into the true fold, persuaded of the true faith, lighted by the true light. The well-known tale of Augustine's wonderful conversion belongs to his life rather than to that of Ambrose.   It was not till two years later, the Easter of 387, that the wanderer was finally received into the Church; and we read with enhanced interest the instruction which Ambrose is then believed to have delivered for the benefit of the catechumens, and especially the exposition of the doctrine of the two sacraments, which is preserved for us under the title "Of the Mysteries."

CHAPTER IX.

CONFLICT WITH THE ARIANS.

A.D. 385–386.

MEANWHILE Justina, who had by this time forgotten, or learnt to undervalue, the loyal services of Ambrose when Maximus was threatening captivity and ruin, began again to display openly her enmity to him and his faith. She demanded that one of the churches in Milan should be surrendered for the use of the Arians. To grant this would have been not to make a charitable concession to the weakness of well-meaning and ignorant brethren, but to give up the authority of the great Council of Nicæa, and of that second Council at Constantinople which had reaffirmed its decisions. It would have been to allow by implication that the point at issue between Arius and Athanasius was of trifling importance, and not of the essence of Christianity. To yield up to the teachers of a half-Christian half-philosophical religionism the buildings so lately won for the preachers of Evangelical truth would have been not a laudable charity, but a culpable indiscretion, if not a surrender of a sacred trust. Valentinian's neglect to remove a heathen altar from the Senate-house had been construed into a tacit admission of the possible truth of the old religion of

the land; what inferences would be drawn from a concession such as Justina required? Ambrose felt, and
all the Catholics felt with him, that the demand must
be resisted to the death.

The greater part of what we know of the ensuing
events we learn from a letter of Ambrose to his sister
Marcellina.

It was now the fifth week in Lent, 385, and it seems
to have been the object of the empress to make
Easter a day of triumph over the Catholics. A
definite demand was made on her part, in the name
of her son the emperor, for the Portian *basilica*, or
church, outside the city walls (now called by the name
of St. Victor). Subsequently the "new" church,
within the walls, a larger and more convenient struc-
ture (now known as St. Nazaro Maggiore), was asked
for, though this latter claim does not seem to have been
pressed. The demand was made by officers of state,
purporting to act for the emperor; but Ambrose replied
that God's priest could not surrender God's temple.

On Palm Sunday the bishop had completed the
earlier duties in the "old" church, and was proceeding with the Communion service, when news was
brought that the Portian church had been seized, and
that the state curtains, surrounding the place of honour
occupied by the imperial family, had been placed
there as a sign of its being in the possession of
Justina; that the people were flocking to the place,
and had laid hold of Castulus, an Arian presbyter, to
whom they were not unlikely to do violence. Much
shocked at this, he interrupted the sacred office by
sending some clergy to rescue the man, and by a

private prayer that no blood—save his own, if that were needful—might be shed.

Severe punishments, both by way of fine and imprisonment, were inflicted on a number of wealthy tradesmen who had taken part in the tumult, or were accused of so doing. They all professed themselves ready to suffer twice as much for their Church. The people about the court were enjoined not to appear in public, and such threats were used that a terrible persecution seemed near at hand. Again Ambrose was asked to surrender the church : again he refused. "It is not mine to give—all that is mine belongs to the poor. It is not the emperor's, for it belongs to God."

Troops were sent under arms to occupy the church ; and it seems as if from the first the fidelity of the orthodox soldiers to their heretical mistress was more than suspected, since a contingent of Goths, who were Arians, formed part of the detachment. Ambrose passed the whole of one day, apparently Tuesday in Holy Week, in the church, dreading lest blood should be shed, so strong was the feeling of the people. At night he went home to rest, but returned to his post on the Wednesday before sunrise. He found the church surrounded with soldiers, but their behaviour was quiet, and many of them made no secret of their attachment to him and the Catholic cause. The service of the day had commenced, when he learnt that another church, the "new basilica," was filled with people, who implored him to come to them. He remained, however, where he was, and preached. The lessons of the day were from the

Book of Job, and he took occasion to speak of the
Christian virtues of faith and patience, commending
the people for their gentleness, so like that of Job,
and their faithful reply to the imperial menaces and
censures: "We do not fight, your Majesty, and we do
not fear, we only make our prayer." Then he showed
how the trials that beset Job had been permitted to
come upon him their pastor; the tempter had endeavoured to rob him of his spiritual heritage and his
spiritual children. Last of all, in the spirit of that
famous sermon which John Chrysostom preached
some eighteen years later against an empress, he in-
veighed against Justina in a way which scarcely com-
mends itself to our taste. " All the worst trials that
have assailed God's people have come through
women. Job's wife tempted him, saying, 'Curse God
and die,' and a woman now bids me, ' Give up the
altar of God.' So Eve led Adam astray, Jezebel per-
secuted Elijah, and Herodias compassed the death of
John the Baptist." As the sermon proceeded, it was
announced to him (though, as it turned out, without
foundation) that the imperial curtains had been
removed from the Portian church, a token of yielding on the part of his opponents. " How wonderful,"
he burst out, " are the dealings of God ! We have
this day sung in the Psalms ' O God, the heathen are
come into Thine inheritance.' Heathen and Goths,
and men of many a tribe and race, have come into
Thine inheritance, and seized on Thy temple. But
many of them have remained there : many of those
who came to invade the inheritance have been made
with us the heirs of God; 'there brake He the arrows

of the bow, the shield, the sword, and the battle.'"
He was pressed to go to one of the other churches,
but he still declined; he sent, however, some presbyters to the Portian church, imagining that the
emperor had withdrawn his mother's claim.   But he
was disappointed to find himself shortly after taken to
task by a messenger from the palace, who taxed him
with "tyranny."   "I would not go myself to the
church," was his reply, "but I sent my presbyters,
because I believed that the emperor had at last come
round to our side.   As to priestly tyranny, all that I
am guilty of is expressed in the words, 'When I am
weak, then am I strong.'   The ministers of God have
often endured, but never practised, tyranny."

That night was passed in the church, for egress
was prevented by the soldiers.   Like St. Paul in
prison, the brethren spent their time in reciting psalms
and hymns.   Next morning (Maundy Thursday)
Ambrose preached on the effects of penitence, from
the book of Jonah, which was read in the lessons for
the day.   He had scarcely concluded when the
welcome news came that the soldiers were withdrawn
from the churches, and the sentences passed a few
days before remitted.   The people, soldiers and
civilians alike, testified their joy in the most lively
manner.   At least that Easter was to be spent in
peace, though Ambrose foresaw troubles yet to come.
One of the ushers of the court, Calligonus, sent him
an insolent message, threatening to cut off his head
for opposing the emperor.   Ambrose's reply shows
how little he cared for these and similar menaces: he
considered them, Theodoret says, as mere bugbears

to frighten children with : " I hope you may be able to carry out your threat. I will suffer like a bishop, and you may act the part of an usher."

He was right in supposing that the question was not yet settled. The apparent triumph of the orthodox only incensed Justina the more, just as their victory at Sirmium had done five years before. In 386 she extorted from Valentinian an edict to the effect that the Arians should be legally recognised, and, as a necessary consequence, be permitted to occupy some at least of the churches; and that it should be a capital offence to presume to oppose them, either publicly, or by presenting petitions against them. The prime mover in this matter, and no doubt the chief adviser of Justina, was a man of indifferent character and savage disposition, a Skythian by birth, named Auxentius. He was recognised by the Arians of Milan as their bishop, but for convenience, and to avoid unpopularity with the Catholics, had ceased to call himself Auxentius, since that name brought with it the recollection of the Arian predecessor of Ambrose, and adopted the name Mercurinus. The usual instructions for drawing out the edict were placed in the hands of the chief secretary, Benevolus, who, though not yet baptized, was an orthodox catechumen. He expressed unwillingness to prepare such a document, and was forthwith deprived of his office, and compelled to retire from Milan to Brescia, while a more accommodating minister was put into his place.

The empress and her adviser also induced the young emperor to send Dalmatius, one of his officers, to Ambrose, desiring him either to quit the city, or consent to meet Auxentius and dispute with him in the imperial consistory before a certain number of arbitrators or jurymen (*judices*) to be chosen by the two disputants. He declined to accept either alternative, and on being termed "contumacious" by Dalmatius, addressed a respectful, but firm and dignified, remonstrance to the emperor himself. "It was distinctly laid down as a principle," he said, "by your august father, Valentinian I., that in matters of faith and ecclesiastical order, priests should be tried by priests. Are the laity to assume the right of judging bishops? Will your Clemency take upon yourself to do what your father deliberately asserted to be beyond his authority when he said, 'It is not mine to judge between bishops'?" And here he reminded the emperor that, being still unbaptized, he could hardly claim to pronounce sentence respecting a faith which had not yet been fully imparted to him. As to the disputation with Auxentius, whom he himself did not recognise as a bishop, he respectfully refused to hold any; first, because he had no confidence in the persons whom he proposed to appoint as his arbitrators—the emperor had excused himself from giving their names; they might be—indeed there was every reason to believe that some of them really were—heathens or Jews : next, because the people, as far as they were concerned, had already decided the matter when they chose him (Ambrose) to be their bishop : and thirdly, because such a dispute would in effect be inconsistent with the new law, which forbad any opposition being offered to the Arians. If Auxentius chose to appeal to a synod, he would be there in his place as Bishop of Milan, but he did not feel it consistent with the dignity of his sacred office to appear before the emperor's consistory; he had once, indeed, appeared before such a tribunal, but that was as an envoy on the emperor's behalf (it was when he went to treat with Maximus); he could not consent to undergo a trial before him. And he was determined not to leave the city. In past time he was always to be found, and could easily have been dismissed; to retire now would be in effect to abandon his flock, and to surrender his charge. "Could I be sure that my church would not be handed over to the Arians, I would gladly place myself at the disposal of your Piety; but if I alone am in your way, how is it that not my church only, but all others, are threatened with aggression?"

Such was the spirited reply which Valentinian, or rather Justina, received to the demand conveyed to the intrepid bishop. Meanwhile, precautions had been taken by the Catholics to prevent the occupation of any of the sacred buildings by the Arians without the employment of force. By the direction of their pastors the people assembled in the churches, and remained in them all day and all night, relieving one another, of course, in turn, and passing the time in the recitation of psalms and the singing of hymns. Some of the latter were from the pen of Ambrose himself, and were objected to as "deceiving" the people, they spoke so distinctly of the ever-blessed Trinity in Unity. We may presume the well-known " *Æterna Christi munera*," with its bold ring and its distinct Trinitarian doctrine, to have been one of them.

The mode adopted in reciting the Psalms was that which we term antiphonal, or alternating from side to side. This mode was copied from the practice of the Eastern Church. It was the fashion among the Jews; we find a trace of responsory chanting in Exod. xv. 21,— "Miriam answered them," where the original language shows that "them" (masculine) refers to the men who had just uttered their choral song; and in 1 Sam. xviii. 7, the women "answered" one another as they played; and we gather from Ezra iii. 11, and Nehem. xii. 40, that it became the settled order in the second Temple. The Eastern Christians no doubt learnt this mode of reciting the Psalter from the Jewish ritual, and Ambrose, as prelate of a Church which seems to have had closer connection with Greece than other Western churches, very naturally at this conjuncture adopted the Oriental use, which continued in after-times to be that of the Church of Milan. The Milanese ritual still retains some of its original peculiarities; the general practice of antiphonal chanting has spread from northern Italy over the whole of the West.

Ambrose not only taught his flock at this time to chant the Psalms, but also instructed them from the Psalter. It is most probable that his remarks on the cxixth Psalm were sermons delivered during this period of trouble.

The occupants of the churches, though not actually imprisoned within them, were kept in some sort of restraint by a cordon of armed men thrown round each building; and some alarm having been caused by a rumour or a fancy that these guards were likely to proceed to violence, and still more by the report

that their bishop was about to comply with the
Imperial request, and leave the city (an attempt to
arrest him they had already defeated by a demonstration of force), Ambrose took occasion at once to
calm their anxiety and to exhort them to firmness
by a sermon which he addressed to them on a day,
probably Palm-Sunday, when one of the New Testament lessons told of our Lord's entry into Jerusalem,
and one of those from the Old Testament was the
very appropriate passage containing the account of
Ahab's dealing with Naboth of Jezreel. " I am not
ntending to desert you," he said : " it is my custom
to show all due deference to a secular emperor, but,
in such a case as the present, not to surrender. I
fear neither threats nor sufferings ; they are but temptations from the Evil One ; and the Lord, who
'hath need' of us, as He had of the creature we
have just read of in the lesson, will help us not to
give way. Remember how Elisha's servant, when his
eyes were opened, saw the troops of angels round
himself and his master ; remember how the angel
was sent to St. Peter in the prison. But our lot may
be to suffer." And here the preacher adds that
apocryphal story of St. Peter's last hours at Rome, so
familiar to us from the striking picture of Caracci.
" After his triumph over Simon Magus, Peter excited
the jealousy of the heathen by his preaching, and
was entreated by the Christians to withdraw from the
city for a time, lest he should be seized and taken
from them. He left Rome accordingly by night.
Scarcely had he emerged from the city gate when he
saw the Lord coming to meet him. Astonished, he

asked, as he had once asked before, 'Lord, whither goest Thou?' (*Domine, quo vadis?*) 'I am coming,' said the Divine Master, 'to be crucified again.' Peter knew that Christ could not suffer again, for 'in that He died, He died unto sin once, but in that He liveth, He liveth unto God.' He felt that the second crucifixion must be not in His Own Person, but in the person of His servant, and forthwith returned to Rome, to glorify the Lord Jesus by his own death on the cross. So too, it may be, the Lord requires us to suffer with Him. Come what may, our answer to the demand of Auxentius will be that of Naboth in our lesson to-day, 'The Lord forbid it me that I should give the inheritance of my fathers unto thee,' the inheritance of Dionysius, Eustorgius, Myrocles, and all the confessors and martyrs who have preceded me here. How well, too, the other lesson of to-day suits us in our present condition! The Jews, we read, would have bid the Lord silence the children who were uttering His praises; and He would not, but went on, and cast the worldly out of the House of God. So when we utter the praises of Christ, our heretical opponents are wroth, and threaten us with pains and death : worse than the Gadarenes who could not bear the presence of Christ, these men are furious even against His praises. But Auxentius and his crew, who would drive out the faithful with the sword, shall feel, not the sword indeed, but the scourge of the Lord. You, brethren, know the truth that Christ is God, and will maintain it against the vile synod of Ariminum that pronounced Him a creature, and against the Arians, who are for rendering unto Cæsar

not the tribute due to him, which we are ready to pay
to the full, but the houses of God. A faithful emperor
is a son of the Church, but he is not lord over her."

With such unshaken firmness on the part of bishop
and people, it is not surprising that the Imperial party
perceived themselves to be in a weak minority, and
gave way. The Catholics, too, met with support
from an unexpected and influential quarter, such as
we may imagine they did not care for, and in a form
they would be disposed to deprecate. But it probably
had a great effect, nevertheless. The emperor Maximus, the usurping emperor, if that term may be
employed where there is no constitution and no rule
of succession, intimated to Valentinian his strong
disapproval of the measures taken against Ambrose,
and the manner in which he was being treated, recommending the emperor to follow the example and
abide by the faith of his father; and hinted that
unless matters in this respect were altered for the
better, he himself might find it necessary to march
upon Milan. As we might expect, the persecution
of the orthodox, and of Ambrose in particular, came
to a sudden termination. The action of Maximus
was not entirely disinterested; he wanted a cause of
complaint and a pretext for war, and was guided by
motives of policy quite as much as by a keen sense
of justice; but one conceives a certain respect for
him, not merely as having been (whether sincerely or
not) a champion of the true faith, but as having been
able to see the greatness of Ambrose's character, and
as having had the magnanimity to espouse the cause
of one who had so freely pleaded with him and so
dauntlessly withstood him.

CHAPTER X.

CHURCH-BUILDING.—MAXIMUS AND JUSTINA.

A.D. 386–387.

THE reverence with which Ambrose was regarded was soon after enhanced by a circumstance which was considered at the time as a proof of Divine favour,—the discovery of the bodies of the martyrs Gervasius and Protasius. He had been requested to consecrate a new church in the same manner as one which he had not long before solemnly dedicated—the "Roman basilica," as it was called, from being situated near the Roman gate of Milan. "To do this," he said, "I must find the remains of martyrs"; for the prevailing custom then was to build churches, if possible, over the tombs of those who had died for the faith, or else, when they were built, to hallow them by placing some martyr's earthly frame to rest within them. Search had to be made, nor did it seem likely to be rewarded, for Mediolanum had not been fruitful in martyrs. The bishop was led to desire an excavation to be made in front of the chancel of the church of SS. Felix and Nabor, otherwise called St. Philip's. It is still in existence, though not used as a place of worship. There were found the remains of two tall men, the skeletons quite complete, surrounded by a quantity of blood. A corrupt practice had arisen,

which later ages have only too faithfully copied, of breaking up such relics into fragments, carrying them about,
and disposing of them for money; and a law against
so doing was enacted by Theodosius in this very year.
These bodies were not so treated : they were carefully
embalmed and preserved entire, and were conveyed
for the night to the church of Fausta (now the chapel
of St. Satyrus).   There they were watched, and the
next day transferred to the new church, close at hand,
which was called by the name of Ambrose himself.
As they passed, a blind man received his sight.

Such is the account given by Ambrose in a letter to
his sister Marcellina.   The main points are repeated
by St. Augustine, who adds what Ambrose himself
stated in two sermons, of which he gives his sister a
sketch, that many cures were effected and many evil
spirits cast out by the instrumentality of the holy
martyrs.

The bodies were identified as those of Gervasius
and Protasius, two Milanese, who had suffered three
centuries before, in the time of Nero or Domitian.
Their place of burial had been forgotten, till the discovery of their remains brought it to the recollection
of some old people, who remembered having heard
their names and read the inscription on their tomb.

The Arian party denied the bodies to be those of
martyrs at all, and derided the idea of miraculous
cures, accusing the bishop of having hired men to
personate demoniacs and to feign themselves to have
been healed of diseases.   Ambrose, however, writes
apparently with the most perfect sincerity and good
faith; Augustine and Paulinus evidently believed most

implicitly in the truth of the whole story. The latter is no doubt a credulous writer : the life, or rather the memoir, of Ambrose, which we have under his name, contains a number of marvels, which are due to a loving but decidedly uncritical imagination. In this case, however, he expresses himself as if from personal knowledge. The man who received his sight was named, he tells us, Severus, and was often seen by him in later times as a constant worshipper in the Ambrosian church. He says he was cured on touching the dress of the martyrs. Augustine, who writes as an eyewitness, tells us that the man was well known to all the citizens, and that he recovered his sight on applying to his eyes a handkerchief with which he had been permitted to touch the bier on which the holy relics lay.

The affectionate interest with which the early Church regarded the earthly remains of holy men, and especially of martyrs, is scarcely intelligible to us : we identify it with the thick crust of error which has grown up in the Roman Church around the doctrine of the communion of saints and the state of the departed. We shrink from a history which, thanks to papal perversion of the truth, seems to introduce us to a superstitious, if not idolatrous, veneration of a decaying creature. But what seems idolatry and superstition in the nineteenth century, after the false teachings of the thirteenth and the reaction of the sixteenth, was not necessarily such in the fourth, any more than the free expressions of an Ante-Nicene writer about the Son of God prove him to have held the doctrine of Arius.

We are, moreover, naturally reluctant to give credence to accounts of post-apostolic miracles. They are not needed by us, says St. Chrysostom, nor ought we to be grieved that we do not see them : they were given for those that did not believe. So we habitually reject each story as a whole, instead of criticising the alleged miracle as such. In this case so distinct are the expressions of Ambrose and his disciples, that we cannot imagine them to have been simply mistaken, still less to have been deceived by a series of cleverly-arranged tricks; and we are forced either to admit that things did happen much as they describe, or else to believe, with the Arians and Gibbon, that the great bishop of Milan was guilty of an impious fraud ; that he not only wrote to his sister, but also in solemn words, and in the name of his Master, asseverated, in a consecrated place, and before a company of Christians, what he and many of them knew to be an absolute falsehood ; and that he either deceived those whom he taught, or persuaded them to conspire with him in bearing testimony to the lie which he had devised. Whether we consider the occurrence to have been really miraculous or not, is quite another question. Without pronouncing decisively for or against the credibility of miracles later than A.D. 100, we may at least suggest that we have here the account of some exceptional phenomena, unscientifically given. Those who think it more likely that a Christian bishop should, with the connivance and approbation of other Christians, invent, solemnly assert, and propagate, a wicked untruth, than that cures apparently miraculous should have been wrought as described, will of course

reject the whole tale ; while those who admire the
straightforward honesty of Augustine's treatise *De
Mendacio* will be disposed to think that he at least
believed, and felt assured that the teacher whom he
so revered believed also, what they have both recorded :
and that they, and Christian people generally, did
actually look upon what happened as a testimony
from above in favour of the martyrs, and, inferentially,
in favour of the Catholic doctrine.

The Paschal tide both of 385 and 386 had been a
time of alarm and disquiet for Ambrose. That of the
next year[1] (387) was marked by a very different
event—the baptism of his spiritual scholar Augustine,
with his son Adeodatus, and his friend Alypius.
Tradition, which has been over-busy with the lives of
the saints, converting legend into history till history
is mistaken for legend, has introduced here a story
we could well wish it were possible to believe—that
the glorious " Te Deum " was composed by bishop
and neophyte in a burst of ecstasy immediately after
the performance of the sacred rite, and chanted
alternately by them as they returned from the baptistery to their places in the church. But it cannot
have been. It is interesting that Augustine mentions
the effect produced on him by the church music
which Ambrose had introduced the year before ; and
there is very little doubt, also, that it is to the period
of preparation of the catechumens of this year that
we must refer, besides other treatises, the short but

---

[1] There is some doubt whether this date be the correct one ;
but the chronology which fixes the event to this year in preference to 386 or 388 (Baronius) seems the most consistent.

weighty exposition of the doctrine of the two sacraments which we know by the title "On the Mysteries."

It was not long after this that Ambrose was once
more called upon to appear in the character of a
statesman. Maximus, who had for the past three
years been observing with tolerable fidelity the com-
pact made with the Emperors Theodosius and Valentinian after Gratian's death, repeated the intimation,
which he had not long before given under the pretext
of espousing the cause of Ambrose and orthodoxy, of
an intention to enter Italy and take the government
of the West into his own hands. Ambrose was des-
patched, as he had been in 383, to endeavour to
prevent the invasion. He expected a private au-
dience, as a mark of respect at once to his imperial
master's rank and his own episcopal dignity. This
being refused him, he declined to accept the saluta-
tion offered him by the would-be emperor, complain-
ing of the discourtesy which had compelled him to
transact his business in the public consistory. Maximus, in his turn, complained bitterly of him as having, in
conjunction with Bauto (a Frank general in the Roman
service, who had been consul in 385, and whose
daughter was the well-known Eudoxia, wife of Arcadius,
and persecutor of St. Chrysostom), deceived him,
and prevented his pushing his first success. Ambrose
calmly pointed out that this charge was futile ; that
he had been guilty of no deception, and that all he,
and Bauto too, had done, was loyally to defend the
interests of the youthful emperor who had been
entrusted to their guardianship. He also renewed
his petition for the delivery of the body of Gratian ;

and finally made an emphatic protest against the cruel treatment of the Priscillianists, refusing to hold communion with Ithacius, Idacius, and the other bishops who had procured the capital punishment of Priscillian. Though he had grievously erred from the faith, his error did not justify the torture and death of himself and his misguided followers.

The diplomacy of Ambrose was this time unsuccessful. Abruptly dismissed, he forthwith quitted Trèves, where the interview had taken place, and returned to Milan, where he warned the young emperor not to trust the usurper, but to exercise the utmost circumspection in dealing with him. Valentinian, however, thought that another might succeed where the bishop had failed, and sent a second embassy in the person of Domninus, a man of Syrian extraction and one of his officers. This man was, with flattery and presents, easily cajoled by Maximus, who persuaded him that he (Maximus) was likely to prove a good friend to the emperor, and actually induced him to take some troops back with him, under pretence of giving aid against a barbarian raid on Pannonia. The envoy, instead of checking, really facilitated the passage of the Alps ; and so completely had the plans of the invader been organized, that an army followed hard upon his footsteps, and appeared unexpectedly before the walls of Milan.

Justina had obstinacy enough to defend a heresy and to persecute an orthodox prelate, but not sufficient nerve or courage to confront an invader and fight for an empire. On the appearance of the army from Gaul, she and Valentinian withdrew to Aquileia.

Even this retreat did not seem secure. Embarking at one of the ports of Istria, they sailed through the Adriatic, and rounding the shores of Greece, ultimately reached Thessalonica, one of the principal seaports of the Eastern Empire. The flight of the emperor and his mother seemed to absolve his subjects from their allegiance, and at all events put an end to that personal bond of union between governor and governed which is so powerful in preserving an hereditary monarchy, and so indispensable to an elective empire. The Westerns submitted to Maximus without a struggle. But a terrible time followed. Piacenza, Modena, Bologna, and not a few other towns and cities were taken, spoiled, and partly overthrown, and many of their inhabitants made captive. Ever active in doing good, Ambrose exerted himself to procure means of ransom for these miserable sufferers, and even went so far as to break up and sell the sacred vessels of the churches to procure the necessary funds. This proceeding was made the ground of strong objection to him by the Arian party, but defended by his friends, and notably by Augustine.

Maximus, meanwhile, endeavoured to get the Bishop of Rome on his side, and accordingly wrote Siricius, who had succeeded Damasus in 384, a letter, in which he professed the utmost respect for him and his clergy and a deep attachment to the Catholic faith. But that prelate was as wise as Ambrose, and possibly had had the benefit of his counsel. Maximus did not gain him as an adherent; and a decree was shortly afterwards issued restoring the idols which had been removed by the late emperor : the invader, having failed to secure the Catholics, made a bid for the heathen.

The capture of Milan was the last event of magnitude in the life of Justina. Worn out by the fatigues of her flight, or broken down by disappointment and shame, or overcome by exasperation at knowing that Ambrose had escaped her, and was thenceforth to be a power in Milan, she breathed her last in the middle of the next year (388) ; whether in exile or not is uncertain, but probably in her own home. Ambrose was freed from an implacable foe, the Church from a powerful protector of heresy, and the evil genius of her son and of the Western Empire was no more.

CHAPTER XI.

THEODOSIUS.

A.D. 388.

THERE could be no doubt of the policy which it behoved Theodosius to adopt. The weakness and confusion in which he found his empire in 379, and from which it had not recovered in 383, rendered it then expedient for him to temporize : the strength and order to which he had now brought his dominions made it not only possible but necessary for him to offer a vigorous and decided resistance to the invader of the West. The same ambition which had led Maximus to move from Trèves to Milan, would, if he were not checked and forced to retire, lead him in a few years to push on still further in the same direction; and it would be better to forestall such a movement, and to remove the possibility, rather than have to combat the actuality, of an eastern invasion. Moreover it was an admirable opportunity for satisfying the warlike longings of those barbarian subjects of the Empire who had come from the north of the Danube, and though settled, and as yet tolerably tranquil, were still but half-tamed. To employ their energies in a way congenial to their tastes, and at the same time to lessen their number, was both a safe and a politic measure. And honour and justice led in the same direction. The son of that Valentinian to whom he owed his early advancement, the brother of that Gratian who conferred on him the Imperial dignity, was now a fugitive and a suppliant within his dominions. Could he with honour refuse him the counsel and aid he sought, and stand by and see him dethroned without a single word or blow in his favour?

If we could find that Ambrose at this period had paid a visit to the East, or had written to Theodosius, we might well imagine that the voice which had twice pleaded for Valentinian with the usurper had not been silent before a duly-recognised emperor, and that the Bishop of Milan had urged on the ruler of the East the imperative duty of defending, and the shameful-ness of deserting, his youthful colleague. Ambrose, however, though he appears to have quitted Milan, and found himself secure in that Aquileia which was not a sufficiently safe refuge for the flying empress and her son, does not seem to have gone any farther eastward. His retirement was necessary, owing to the confusion and tumult inseparable from the occupation of a city by troops, even though they were received as friends by the populace, who rather acquiesced in than desired their presence. The bishop himself had in fact nothing to fear, even had he been a man who feared anything : for Maximus was on the side of the orthodox, and, as we have seen, though passionate and ambitious, was powerfully impressed in his favour. Some men under such circumstances might have been induced to take the part of one who was at least a *de facto* sovereign and a probable friend. But Ambrose had tact enough, as a statesman, to see that his was not the winning side : and still more, as a Christian, could not, whatever he might gain by it, entertain the idea of deserting the cause of one who seemed to have been confided to his care.

To the policy and the sense of honour, each of which by itself would have been sufficient to determine Theodosius in his line of action, a third motive was subsequently added. He was a widower : his beloved and saintly wife, Flaccilla (or Placilla, or Placida, for we meet with all three forms of the name) had died in 385, about a year after giving birth to his second son, Honorius. The princess Galla, one of the three daughters of Justina, made an impression on him, which, mainly through the adroitness of her scheming mother, resulted in her becoming his second wife : and so to the other claims which Valentinian had upon him was superadded that of a brother-in-law.

The envoys whom Maximus had sent to treat with him were dismissed with an indecisive answer, for he was not the man to throw away an opportunity by premature disclosures. He made ready secretly, as Maximus himself had done, and when all was ripe for action marched suddenly upon the invader, stimulated and assured of success by an Egyptian ascetic named John, in whom he had great confidence. He took the road to Milan : but all was decided before he reached that city. The troops of Maximus encountered him (August 27) in Pannonia, at Sissek, on the banks of the Save, and again at Pettau, on the Drave, and were almost annihilated : their master fled to Aquileia, while the wretched assassin Andragathias,

who was now commander of the fleet, and had hoped
to become the favoured and confidential minister of
a powerful potentate, flung himself despairing into the
river. The people, who had so readily given up
Valentinian for Maximus, were just as ready to surrender their new lord ; and Ambrose, the loyal friend
of the two emperors, was (probably) there, and, we
may be sure, did not plead the cause of the vanquished
leader, who found himself compelled to fly, and fell
into the hands of the conqueror. He begged to be
allowed to live and become his lieutenant or depen-
dent : and for a while Theodosius seemed inclined
to spare, if not to employ him : but the remembrance
of Gratian was enough to extinguish any lingering
disposition to mercy, and Maximus was surrendered
to the soldiery, who lost no time in putting him to
death. That his followers were treated with the
utmost clemency was due mainly to the entreaties of
Ambrose. The victor with his army entered Milan
in triumph, where he passed the winter, and employed
himself in restoring order to the recovered dominions
of his youthful brother-in-law and colleague ; one of
his first measures being to rescind the order for the
restoration of idols.

He soon found himself brought into collision with
the bishop, who had now returned to his own city,
and was as bold and determined in maintaining what
he conceived to be the interests of the Church against
an orthodox and victorious emperor, as he had been
when contending for the rights of the orthodox with
an heretical and weak-minded empress. In this particular instance, while we admire his frankness, we

cannot but feel that, according to the rules of justice and charity, right was with the instincts of the emperor, whom he opposed and finally over-persuaded.

The Christians in a small town called Fort Callinicus, at no great distance from Aquileia, had, probably during the time of anarchy which must have succeeded the flight of Valentinian, in an outburst of fanaticism burnt a Jewish synagogue which had been erected in the town; and about the same time certain monks in the same place had destroyed a chapel belonging to the Gnostic sect known by the name of Valentinians. The injured parties appealed to the emperor Theodosius, who forthwith ordered that the bishop of the town where the outrage had taken place, who was charged with having instigated it, should see that the synagogue was properly rebuilt; and added that the monks should be punished for what they had done in the matter of the chapel. With our tolerant habits and different modes of thought, we can scarcely understand the commission of the offence, but, supposing it committed, are inclined to consider the Imperial decree to have been most equitable, if not too lenient to the offenders. We can agree with Ambrose in his refusal to surrender churches to the Arians; we cannot understand his taking the part of the rioters of Fort Callinicus. We should applaud a prelate who declined to allow a church in his diocese to be given up for Unitarian worship; but we can hardly imagine the bishop of a country city—say Ely or Bangor—recommending the forcible demolition of a synagogue or a Mormonite meeting-house; or, supposing for a moment his lordship to have been so inconceivably and ridiculously intolerant as to procure such a breach of the peace, we should scarcely expect the archbishop of his province to denounce the natural proposal that he should replace the ruined edifice. But things were different fifteen centuries ago, and in Italy. Ambrose endeavoured to obtain a modification of the emperor's order, and finding his proceedings of no avail, addressed a letter of remonstrance to him. It begins with an apology for doing what he felt to be his duty in expostulating, and a not undeserved commendation of the fairness and kindness of Theodosius. The writer then goes on to express his entire approval of the action of the bishop, and to avow himself ready to take on himself the responsibility of the deed, in terms which almost make it seem as if he had really had some share in it. To make a Christian bishop, he argues, replace a building in which Christ is denied, or to punish people for destroying a virtually heathen conventicle, where the thirty-two æons of the system of Valentinus are adored, would be to play the part of a second Julian, and to let Jews triumph over God's Church; the synagogue so built might bear the inscription, "Temple of Impiety, erected out of the spoils of Christians." To the argument that setting a house on fire must be always punishable, whatever the character of the house, he dexterously opposes the fact, that not only had no notice been taken of the burning in past years of the houses of several of the prefects at Rome, but that a short time before, when the house of Nectarius, bishop of Constantinople, had been burnt in an Arian riot, Theodosius had been induced by his son Arcadius to overlook what had happened. Finally, he adds, alluding skilfully to the late victory gained by the person he is addressing, the majority of Christians at Rome had prophesied the fall of Maximus because he had published an edict in favour of the Jews under somewhat similar circumstances after the burning of a synagogue at Rome.

The letter is remarkable, as showing the feelings then entertained towards the ancient people of God. To the contempt and aversion felt for them by the Italians, apart from all religious considerations,—a sentiment of which we find abundant proof, for instance, in the Satires of Juvenal, to mention no other writer,—there was added the utter detestation and loathing which every Christian thought it his duty to entertain and express, as though each unfortunate Israelite were personally chargeable with and responsible for the murder of the Prince of Peace; that scorn and hatred which in later times marked out the Jewry and the Ghetto, and produced and won belief for the story of Hugh of Lincoln, and such-like tales of horror and profanation. It is strange to us to find such sentiments not only held and avowed, but gloried in, by a man like Ambrose.

Not satisfied with sending his letter, he took a still more decisive step. A few days after, the emperor, as usual, attended church, and the bishop took occasion to preach a sermon, of which he gives an account, as we saw he did of some previous discourses, in a letter to his sister. The Old Testament lesson of the day was Numb. xvii., the account of Aaron's rod that budded; and the preacher deduced from it the priestly duty of rebuking and power of censure. The New Testament lesson was from St. Luke vii., the story of the forgiven sinner in the house of Simon the Pharisee. "The Church," he went on to say, "has tears to wash the feet of Christ, and hairs to wipe them withal, ointment to pour on them, and kisses to imprint on them; the synagogue, like the proud Pharisee, has none." Then turning to the emperor, he reminded him how many gifts God's providence had bestowed on him, and bade him in return offer water and kisses and ointment to the Body of Christ.

The drift of the sermon was palpable, and not least so to the emperor himself. As Ambrose descended from the pulpit, he exclaimed, "So, my lord bishop, you have been preaching at me this morning!" The bishop was about to celebrate holy communion, but a little dialogue ensued here. Such conversational interludes are permitted in synagogues among us at the present day, but are considered so unseemly in our churches, even after service is over, much more in service time, that we read the story with some surprise. Ambrose replied, "I have not been preaching at you, but rather for your good." "Well," replied the emperor, "my order about the rebuilding of the synagogue by the bishop was a little too severe, but that has been rectified. As to the monks, they are guilty of many offences." On this Timasius, one of the chief officers, who was standing by, began to express himself strongly against the monks, when Ambrose cut him short, telling him bluntly that he was talking to the emperor, not to him; the emperor he knew to be a God-fearing man, he would deal

with him (Timasius) very differently. One would
have thought that enough had now been said on
either side, considering the sacredness of the place
and time, and the rank of the two parties. But
Ambrose still remained standing before the emperor.
At last he said, "Give me some security with regard
to your future action in the matter, that I may be
able to make the oblation with a quiet mind." The
emperor nodded, but said nothing; and still the
pertinacious prelate remained standing. "I will
have the rescript amended," said the emperor. But
Ambrose replied that that would not do for him; the
whole proceedings must be quashed, so that there
might be no possibility of the Christians sustaining
any injury. The emperor promised it should be so,
but the bishop was not satisfied till he had heard the
formula equivalent to "On my sacred word and
honour" (*Age fide mea*). These words were at last pronounced, and Ambrose proceeded to the holy table.

This was not the only rebuff that Theodosius
received, and, to his great credit, received without
resenting, at the hands of Ambrose during the early
part of his stay in Italy. He valued the man's in-
flexibility in the discharge of what he felt to be his
duty, and saw clearly that such a faithful and intrepid
servant of his God and of his Church would be a
loyal adherent to his emperor. Fidelity to the Church
has been by some thought incompatible with loyalty
to the State, so that one's duty to God is best dis-
charged by resisting the powers ordained of Him;
and, conversely, stanch Churchmen have been held
open to the charge of being disobedient subjects.

This was evidently not the view either of Theodosius or Ambrose.

It was the custom in Constantinople that the emperor, after making his offering at the holy table, remained with the clergy in the sanctuary. On a certain great festival (probably Christmas, 388[1]) which occurred during his stay in Milan, Theodosius went up and made his offering, and having done so, remained, as he had been accustomed to do, where he was. But the archdeacon was soon sent to desire him to depart from the place assigned to clergy alone, and to show him a post of honour without, not within, the holy place. "The purple," remarked the bishop, "makes princes, but not priests." Ambrose's admonition seems to have had a strong effect, for on his return to Constantinople more than three years later, Theodosius, being invited as usual to continue in the sanctuary, declined to do so, adding a strong expression of approval of the conduct of the Milanese prelate, who had taught him the difference between a prince and a minister of the Church.

---

[1] The affair is by some placed two years later, and at the time of the emperor's readmission to communion, but it more probably occurred at this time.

CHAPTER XII.

THE SIN AND PENANCE OF THEODOSIUS.

A.D. 389–390.

IN the early spring of the year 389 the two emperors removed from Milan, and entered in triumph the ancient capital of the Roman Empire. Short work was made with those relics of heathenism which the tolerance or weakness of preceding Christian emperors had allowed to remain. Symmachus pleaded for the altar of Victory; but as he had not long before written a panegyric on Maximus, his advocacy rather damaged his cause. Statues of gods were thrown down, the pagan temples and chapels, said to amount to 424 in number, were closed, the privileges of the pontifices, flamines, and all the idolatrous hierarchy abolished, and the offering of sacrifices forbidden : a special commission was given to certain officers of rank to search out and seize all instruments of idolatry, and to confiscate all heathen endowments for the use of the emperor, the army, or the church. An appeal for their restoration, supported by not a few Christians, was made to Valentinian ; but he absolutely refused to listen to it. An edict which followed in the next year was even more stringent in its character. Any one offering sacrifice, or divining by entrails, was declared guilty of high treason, and liable to capital punishment; the minor offence of using other pagan observances was forbidden under pain of forfeiture of the building where the rite was performed, or of a heavy fine.

While Theodosius was thus busily employed in sweeping away all traces of religion other than that of the Christian Church, the bishops were turning their attention to the internal condition of the Church, and waging war against heresy and heterodoxy, as the emperor was extirpating idolatry. Jovinian, an Italian monk, a native either of Milan or Rome, and at one time an inmate of a monastery maintained at Milan by Ambrose, had broached certain opinions, which, though we should entirely agree with some of them, and consider others permissible, were by no means in accordance with the general feeling of the majority of Christians of the time. Those who contradict, with whatever truth, the current opinions of their own day, are often betrayed into maintaining, and still more often accused of maintaining, some directly erroneous propositions. Wiclif, and Luther, and Ridley, and Wesley, said and wrote things that might better have been left unsaid and unwritten; and were charged with saying and writing and doing much more, which in their hearts they utterly rejected and abhorred. Jovinian was no exception to the rule. Himself unmarried, and of abstemious, if not ascetic, habits, he held that celibacy and fasting were not in themselves meritorious, and that the married life was as holy as the unmarried; that all sins, as such, were equal in the sight of God; and that all future rewards, as due only to the merits of Christ, would be equal also. To these propositions he added, or was said to have added, an indiscreet expression about the Virgin Mary, and the doctrine that one could not sin after baptism. For this he was styled a Manichæan, a blasphemer, a wolf howling in the fold of Christ. One does not see anything wolfish or blasphemous even in his erroneous theories; and as to Manichæism, his depreciation of asceticism was opposed to Manichæan theory, certainly; though, according to Augustine, the practice of the Manichæans of the time was inconsistent with their principles, being extremely lax and immoral.

Siricius, who had, as has been already mentioned, succeeded Damasus as Bishop of Rome five years before, held a synod of Roman clergy, which declared Jovinian's teaching heretical, and excommunicated him, with eight of his followers. The accused, who had up to this time been living at Rome, then removed to Milan, where their opinions had been first published. The Bishop of Rome immediately sent three of his presbyters with a letter addressed to the Church of Milan, announcing the Roman decision and sentence. The letter, it may be observed, contains no trace whatever of any assertion of Papal authority. The Milanese clergy soon met in synod, and repeated the condemnation pronounced at Rome. The epistle sent to Siricius in reply to his own, salutes him as a brother (not as Vicar of Christ or Head of the Universal Church), examines and answers some of Jovinian's teachings, and announces the excommunication of their author and his adherents by an unanimous vote of the Milanese synod. The (so-called) heresy, Augustine remarks, was soon repressed, and became extinct, never having gone beyond the perversion of a few priests.

The organization of the West was a longer task than Theodosius had calculated on. Instead of being able to return to Constantinople within a few months from the death of Maximus, it was more than three years before he thought it safe—and even then he was mistaken—to entrust the reins of government to a mere youth like Valentinian, however promising, upright, and energetic. His absence from his own dominions was far from being without its effect. Personal rule requires that the personal presence of the ruler should be continually felt; his absence can hardly be compensated even by the ablest of lieutenants. The protracted stay of Theodosius in Rome and Milan was indirectly the cause of a terrible tragedy.

The people of Thessalonica, an important and populous seaport and metropolis of the province of Illyria, already well known to us as the refuge of Valentinian and Justina, were on bad terms with the magistrates of their city; but their ill-temper had for a time vented itself in words rather than deeds. Botheric, a Goth, the commander of the garrison, had, in the early part of 390, imprisoned for a gross offence one of the most popular charioteers of the circus. The devotion of the Thessalonians to the chariot-race was as entire as that of the people of Rome or Constantinople; and the populace on the day of the games lamented the absence of their favourite, and clamoured for his release. Botheric

was inflexible. Enraged by his stern refusal, and
already fancying themselves to have grounds for dissatisfaction with the ruling powers, they burst into
open rebellion, seized him and several of his officers,
murdered them brutally, and dragged their corpses
about the streets. Tidings of the riot were brought
to Milan. The Spanish blood of Theodosius was
roused at the news, and he began to threaten the
direst vengeance against the guilty city. But Ambrose was at his side, and succeeded in calming his
excitement for the time, and obtaining from him a
promise that the affair should be calmly and judi-
cially dealt with. Unhappily, however, the bishop
was required to preside at a synod which sat to
repeat formally the solemn protest which he had
already made before Maximus against the cruelty of
Ithacius, bishop of Sossuba, towards the Priscillianist
heretics. During his absence other counsellors came
to the emperor's side. They roused his fiery temper
by sensational accounts of the Thessalonian outrage,
and argued that lenity would be misplaced and dangerous; it might be construed into a confession of
weakness, and instead of exciting admiration of his
calmness and justice, would only tend to inspire the
disloyal and excitable people of the East with the
hope of further impunity for still more grievous
offences. In an evil moment—for it was the work
of a short time—he yielded to the promptings of his
own choleric disposition and his evil advisers, and
sent orders that the people (assembled in the circus)
should be put to the sword.

The decree, unfairly obtained, was treacherously

executed. Not a word of the coming punishment was breathed in the doomed city. A fresh exhibition of games was announced, and, in order to make the number of victims as large as possible, the whole people were invited to witness it in the name of the emperor. Absence, it was hinted, would be considered as an intentional mark of disrespect. Anxious to stand well in his good graces after what had happened to incense him, the Thessalonians crowded to the circus. Botheric's troops were ready : always greedy of blood, they now thirsted for vengeance also. The signal was given, and no games began, but a promiscuous massacre. Before the sun had set, seven thousand at least—some said more than double the number—of all ages, sexes, stations, and nationalities were lying silent in death ; mown down, says Theodoret, like ears of corn at harvest-time. A counter order eventually arrived from the emperor. It put an end to the slaughter, but could not resuscitate the victims.

The dreadful news was communicated to Ambrose in a letter from Anysius, the successor of his sainted friend Ascholius in the bishopric of Thessalonica. It is a curious specimen of the rhetorical and inflated epistolary style then in vogue. After giving Ambrose to understand that a terrible blow had been struck at their happiness and prosperity, the good bishop goes on to entreat his kind offices with the emperor in favour of the afflicted city: " for certain abandoned and accursed men, tools of the devil, have torn her locks and brought the baldness of reproach on her head. She who once was beautiful and well-favoured, with joyous eyes like Rachel, is now tender-eyed, like Leah, with affliction; she who was of good address, is now covered with shame; she who was free of speech in joy, is now silent in disgrace; she who once sheltered strangers, is now stripped bare by strangers. And if Rachel now weeps at seeing all her children slain, it is said to her, 'How is the faithful city Zion become an harlot!' But she cries aloud to you, father, from afar, like the woman of Canaan; she falls down to you, as the woman with the issue of blood to the Saviour, desiring to touch the hem of your dignity: and who can be her helper but your Holiness? Guide the sacred ears of our lords to pity; exhort the pious, supplicate the compassionate, who under the seal of Christ have silenced the Western thunder of tyranny, that they may have mercy on those whom they have saved from the barbarians, that they may rescue the vessel now sinking with all her crew. Let not the devil, who raised the tumult, say, 'I have prevailed!' for even God disregarded not a disobedient and gainsaying people."

Ambrose was overwhelmed with horror at the tragical tale, and confounded at the way in which the emperor had been cajoled into violating his promise; his dismay was shared by the bishops who were with him on the business of the synod. Theodosius was absent from Milan at the time when the news came, but returned a few days after, and in due course of time proceeded to the church at which he usually worshipped. He was met at the door by the indignant prelate, who addressed him in a speech

preserved by Theodoret, which cannot be better exhibited than in the rendering of our own Hooker:—
" Emperor, it seemeth that how great the slaughter is
which thyself hast made thou weighest not; nor, as
I think, when wrath was settled did reason ever call
to account what thou hadst committed.   Notwithstanding, know thou shouldst what our nature is,
how frail a thing and how fading; and that the first
original from whence we have all sprung was the
very dust whereunto we must slide again.   Neither
is it meet that being inveigled with the show of thy
glistering robes thou shouldst forget the imbecility of
that flesh which is covered therewith.   Thy subjects,
O emperor, are in nature thy colleagues; yea, even
in service thou art also joined as a fellow with them.
For there is one Lord and Emperor, the Maker of
this whole assembly of all things.   With what eyes,
therefore, wilt thou look upon the habitation of that
common Lord?   With what feet wilt thou tread upon
that sacred floor?   How wilt thou stretch forth those
hands from which the blood as yet of unrighteous
slaughter does distil?   The body of our Lord all-
holy how wilt thou take into such hands?   How
wilt thou put His honourable Blood unto that mouth,
the wrathful word whereof hath caused against all
order of law the pouring out of so much blood?
Depart, therefore, and go not about by after-deeds
to add to thy former iniquity.   Receive that bond
wherewith from heaven the Lord of all doth give
consent that thou shouldst be tied, a bond which is
medicinable, and procureth health."

The emperor retired, for he knew Ambrose to be

inflexible. He either invited the bishop to meet him, or proposed to visit him himself; but the prelate declined, and addressed to him a letter, to the same effect as his speech. He expresses in it his great personal regard for him, and acknowledges his piety and zeal, but hints in guarded words at his own disappointment in finding that the emperor's natural impetuosity had not been repressed by good counsel. Then he denounces the Thessalonian crime, and declares that penance, public penance, must be done for it, after the example of David. Till it should be done he could not celebrate the Eucharist in his presence. This determination, he declares solemnly, was forced on him in a dream, in which he saw the emperor come to church, and found himself unable to officiate at the holy table.

No reply was made to this letter, nor did either of the parties move for a long time. The bishop had spoken, and it was not for him to take the initiative, or proffer a pardon which was not sought for. He went on with his pastoral work and study, among other things, holding a long conversation with two eminent Persians, who had come to Italy on purpose to visit and confer with him. The imperial offender was perhaps unable to bring himself to a public confession of his fault, or to comply with the terms on which alone he could be admitted to the full privileges of a Christian. His pride revolted at what his conscience told him he deserved; and so, though that conscience was still active, he made no sign. In this way eight months passed, while he remained still at Milan.

Christmas-time now drew near, and all were preparing for the glad celebration of the Saviour's birth,
but the excommunicated emperor sat sorrowful in his
palace. Rufinus, the *magister palatii*—lord steward of
the household we might call him—ventured to ask
the cause of his grief. Theodosius replied with tears,
"You are mocking me, Rufinus; you do not comprehend the nature of my trouble. I am lamenting
my unhappy lot; the holy Church is open to slaves
and beggars, but is shut to me; and heaven is closed
to me, for I remember the words of our Lord which
distinctly say, 'Whatsoever ye shall bind on earth shall
be bound in heaven.'" "Let me run," said Rufinus,
" and persuade the bishop to release you from your
bonds." "You will not be able to do so," replied
the emperor; "I know the justice of his sentence,
and am sure that he will not violate the Divine law out
of respect for Imperial power." Rufinus, however,
eventually succeeded in obtaining leave to make trial
of the bishop. He seems to have treated the matter
all through with considerable levity, and probably did
not conceal his sentiments when he accosted him.
But he received a very different answer from what he
had expected. "You are as impudent as a dog,
Rufinus," said the prelate. "It was you who advised
the horrible massacre, and yet you exhibit no shame;
you neither blush nor tremble, though you have
offered such violence to the image of God." The
lord steward, whose character Ambrose had not
untruly, though rather brusquely, described, persevered in spite of this unfavourable reply, and remarked
that the emperor was coming, and would be there

G

presently. "I warn you," was the answer, "that if he does come, I shall prevent him from entering the sacred portal. If he then chooses to convert his imperial authority into tyranny, I shall gladly receive death at his hand." Rufinus took a thoroughly anti-ecclesiastical view of the affair; he would probably have been happy to do for his master what some eight centuries later our Henry II. is said to have wished his courtiers to do for him to an unaccommodating prelate—"rid him of a proud priest"; and would certainly, if he had dared, have counselled its being done. He did not, however, go so far as this, but simply sent a message to Theodosius telling him of the result of his interview with the bishop, and begging him to remain in the palace. The message was delivered as the emperor was either passing through or transacting business in the Forum. Reluctant as he had felt to submit to the direction of Ambrose, he was still less inclined to be dictated to by his lord steward; and the attempt made to induce him to resist the authority of the spiritual ruler perhaps confirmed him in the intention of submitting to that authority, and hastened its execution. "I will go," he exclaimed, "and receive the chastisement I deserve." Proceeding to the consecrated precincts, he refrained from entering the church, but went into a parlour where the bishop was sitting, and begged for absolution. After the behaviour of Rufinus, it is not surprising that Ambrose looked upon the visit in the light of a menace, and taxed the emperor with tyranny, insolence towards God, and contempt of His laws. But he received an assurance that he was mistaken. "I am come in no

spirit of rebellion against constituted laws, nor am I
intending to force my way through the sacred gates.
I am here to beg that you will grant me release,
remembering the mercy of our common Lord, and
not close against me that door which He opens to
every penitent." The bishop evidently considered
the eight months' delay in making this request as a
contumacious resistance to spiritual authority, and an
obstinate refusal to exhibit or feel anything like true
contrition; and it is far from improbable that men
from the court had expressed themselves to him in a
manner which by no means gave him a just idea of
the drift of Theodosius's thoughts. Those who had
advised the massacre and those who hated Ambrose
would join in using their utmost endeavours to
prevent the emperor from expressing sorrow for his
hasty and cruel order, and in doing all they could to
keep up an impassable breach between him and the
bishop.

The answer to the emperor's humble words was
still a stern one. "What penitence have you been
showing for your great fault? What remedy have
you applied to the incurable wound you have inflicted?" "It is your duty," answered the penitent,
"to prepare the remedies; mine to accept what is
offered me." "Since, then," said Ambrose, "you
allow your temper to act the part of judge, and
permit anger instead of reason to pronounce sentence,
you must make a law which shall render such hasty
orders null and void. When a sentence of death or
confiscation of property is pronounced, let thirty days
elapse before it is put into execution. After this time

has passed, and you have become cool, let your decree be shown to you. You will then be able to decide rationally whether it is just or not. If the latter, then the writing can be destroyed; if the former, it may be ratified. Where the judgment is right, a little delay will do no harm." The emperor consented. The regulation suggested by Ambrose was not new to him; a similar rule had been laid down by Gratian, but had been either forgotten, or not adopted by himself. The necessary document was speedily prepared and signed, and the excommunication was removed. Laying aside every ornament that could mark his rank, Theodosius entered the church with a deep sigh of relief, and fell prostrate on the floor, smiting his breast, and crying, " My soul cleaveth unto the dust : O quicken Thou me according to Thy word "; and with every sign of the profoundest compunction besought and received absolution and readmission to the communion of the Church. To the day of his death he never ceased to deplore his error, and was so watchful over himself and so careful not to offend, that the more he was irritated the more ready he was to pardon ; and offenders were said not to fear, but to wish, to see him angry. Ambrose testified his belief in the sincerity of his repentance by inscribing to him the book he had written in 384, entitled, " The Defence of the Prophet David."

CHAPTER XIII.

EUGENIUS.

A.D. 392–393.

AFTER a stay of more than three years in Italy, the greater part of which time was spent, not at Rome, the old capital of the Republic, but at Milan, which, since the time of Maximian, had become the chief city of the empire, Theodosius hoped it to be safe, and felt it to be high time, for him to return to his own dominions.   Accordingly in the early spring of 392 he took leave of Ambrose (Valentinian was absent in Gaul), and set out for the East.   During the time his youthful colleague (now just twenty years old) was in his company, he had carefully imparted to him sound political instruction; and had combined with it earnest exhortations to adopt the faith of his father and brother, the true Christian faith.   For the memory of his mother Valentinian had probably but little respect; for Theodosius and Ambrose he entertained the deepest reverence.   His Arian leanings, if he ever had any, were soon exchanged for an earnest desire to be admitted to the membership of the Church; and his hatred of idolatry was so decided, as to make many believe that the adherents of the old

religion had been for months engaged in a con-
spiracy against his life. Under these circumstances,
Theodosius had but little apprehension in leaving
Italy. The affairs of religion, he thought, would be
well provided for in the hands of an emperor now
become orthodox, and guided by such a counsellor as
the Bishop of Milan. The Far West, he imagined,
would be little disposed to rise, after the fate of
Maximus; but, to make matters sure, he had appointed
to the post of commander-in-chief of Gaul a Frank
named Arbogastes, a man of great ability and energy,
loud in his protestations of fidelity to his patrons the
emperors. But the appointment was a mistake, and
a fatal one. The Frank, all the while that he seemed
to be holding the unquiet spirits of his province in
check, was secretly playing his own game. The troops
were corrupted, Franks were thrust into the most important military posts, and the loyal Italian servants
of Valentinian gradually eliminated, their places being
filled by friends of his own.

The young emperor had now been residing for some
time at Trèves. So anxious had he become to be
received into the bosom of the Church, that he sent
and repeated a pressing invitation to Ambrose to come
to him and administer the Sacrament of Baptism,
which he was earnestly desirous of receiving at the
hands of one who had been so faithful to, and so highly
valued by, his father and his brother. Partly owing
to the news of some barbarian demonstration on the
Italian frontier, partly from a wish to meet Ambrose
half-way, he left Trèves, and came southward as far
as Vienne. This independent movement, which

betokened an intention to act without consulting
Arbogastes, was by no means satisfactory to that personage, whose intention was to detain his emperor in
a virtual captivity, which might some day be converted
into an actual one. His dissatisfaction was raised to
its utmost height when Valentinian placed in his
hands a formal dismissal from all his offices. Tearing
the document into shreds and flinging them on the
ground, the Frank insultingly replied, "My authority
was not given by you, and you are powerless to take
it from me." Valentinian had inherited the quick
temper which was the death of his illustrious father.
In a transport of pardonable rage he snatched a sword
from one of his guards, and was with some difficulty
prevented from inflicting a mortal wound on his insolent general. An emperor with a will of his own was
not to be tolerated by Arbogastes. A few days after—
it was Whitsun Eve, May 7, 392—Valentinian was
found in his own chamber a corpse. The cause of
death was strangulation, nor was there the faintest
doubt as to the head that planned or the hands which
perpetrated the deed. It was well known that the
chamberlains of the palace had been tampered with,
and by whom. But to the villany of assassination the
barbarian general added the baseness of slander, and
attempted, though without the smallest success, to
persuade men that the pious young emperor was a
suicide. He did not, however, detain the body, as
Maximus had done that of Gratian ; it was conveyed
to Milan, and, after resting in the palace, buried by
the direction of Theodosius. The Bishop of Milan
preached the funeral sermon, or, more correctly

speaking, pronounced the funeral oration. He enlarged on the moral purity of the deceased, his kindness of heart, his devotion to his duty, and deplored the loss sustained by the Christian cause. " Thou wert smitten, O Church, on one cheek, when thou didst lose Gratian: thou hast turned the other, now that Valentinian has been taken from thee." The regret expressed by some that he had died without receiving Baptism, the preacher said, was needless ; he had wished for it, and had sent for him to administer it : there was no reason to doubt that the gift from above which he had longed for was in effect bestowed on him. As the martyrdom of catechumens was always held to supply the place of the external administration of the Sacrament of regeneration, by the baptism of blood, so it might be hoped that the murdered youth was bathed in his own piety and holy desires. There is more of rhetoric in the discourse, and, we may add, more of the dignity of human merit, than is quite suited to the taste of an English churchman : many of the Scriptural allusions are forced and far-fetched ; and we cannot help wondering, as we read the strong encomiums upon the departed, whether Ambrose had forgotten that he of whom he spoke was a few years before not only unbaptized, but an Arian.

Arbogastes was well enough acquainted with the feelings of Romans to be quite aware that he must be satisfied with the power of an emperor without the name. A century and a half had not effaced the remembrance of the brutal Maximin ; and notwithstanding the success and renown of Philip, and Diocletian, and Maximian, whose title to the Roman

name was more than questionable, it was clear that a
German who should attempt to copy him in his reign
over Italians would only be consigned by them to his
fate.   A puppet emperor must be set up, a degenerate
Roman, who would wear the purple and obey his
commander-in-chief.   Such a person was soon found
in Eugenius, the rhetorician, his secretary and master
of the offices.

The new emperor sent without delay to announce
to Theodosius the unfortunate suicide (as he termed
it) of Valentinian.   Theodosius was once again obliged
to temporize, as he had done with Maximus, and for
the same reason.   The unhappy affair of Thessalonica
had shown him the risk he ran in being absent from
his dominions ; and Constantinople itself was far
from being quiet.   He dismissed the envoys with an
equivocal answer, and with the usual gifts of honour,
but at the same time began to prepare for another
civil war.

Eugenius had not long been invested with the
purple when a deputation from the pagan party at
Rome waited upon him to beg for the restoration of
heathen worship and the restitution of heathen endowments.   They were dismissed with an answer in the
negative ; for Eugenius was professedly a Christian.
A second deputation received a similar reply, but either
perceived some tendency to vacillation on the part
of the emperor, or, more probably, got a hint of
some inclination on the part of Arbogastes to favour
their demands.   They persevered, and Eugenius, while
still declining to restore the endowments to the temples,
agreed to present some of them, as a favour, to certain

eminent persons, " of the Gentile observance," as the euphemistic phrase ran ; coupling with this a relaxation of the edicts of Theodosius which forbad all heathen rites and ceremonies.

Not long after, the new ruler of the West crossed the Alps and proceeded to Milan. He had already sent a letter to the bishop to announce his elevation, and to intimate his intention of visiting the capital. To this he received, at first, no answer. Nor did Ambrose await his arrival, but thought it his wisest course to withdraw, as he had done on the approach of Maximus six years before. He first retired to Bologna, and thence to Florence : sending a letter addressed " To the most clement Emperor Eugenius," in which he explained the reason of his previous silence and of his withdrawal from Milan to be the indulgence shown by a Christian ruler to idolatry. The presenting the heathen endowments to individuals was, he said, a mere quibble : it could not deceive any one, least of all God. " Though the Imperial power is great," he wrote, " consider, sire, how great God is : He sees the hearts of all, He questions the inner conscience, He knows everything before it is done, He knows the inmost recesses of your soul. You do not permit yourself to be deceived ; do you try to conceal anything from God ? has this never occurred to your mind ? however pertinacious they were with you, was it not your part, sire, to be all the more pertinacious in your resistance, for the glory of the Most High, the true and living God, and to refuse them what was inconsistent with the Sacred Law ? Who grudges your giving what you choose to others ? we do not pry into

your liberality, nor envy the advantages of others :
but we are interpreters of your faith. How will you
offer your gifts to Christ? Emperor though you are,
you ought to be, all the more, the servant of God.
How will the priests of Christ dispense your gifts?"

The letter, as we might expect, had no effect. It
was more important for Arbogastes to conciliate a
party at Rome than to procure the doubtful advantage
of the bishop's residence at Milan : he boasted, we
are told, to some Frankish chiefs of being the prelate's
intimate acquaintance and dear friend : but this was
only because of the exalted idea they entertained of
his power ; the wily barbarian had no objection to be
thought to stand in amicable relations to one whose
friendship was supposed to ensure victory : but he did
not want him in the capital. Nor did Eugenius care
to have one near him who would be continually
warning him of the sinfulness of tolerating idolatry,
and by whose orders he had already been denied the
privilege of worshipping in the churches. So Ambrose
still remained at Florence ; unwilling, he said, to be
near one who had mixed himself up with sacrilege.
Nor was he an unwelcome guest. Like his own
Milanese flock, the Tuscans were charmed with his
preaching.

CHAPTER XIV.

VICTORY AND DEATH.

A.D. 394–395.

THE preparations of Theodosius were at last complete, and on January 10, 394, he began to move westwards. Eugenius and Arbogastes set out from Milan to meet him, fulminating dire threats against the Christians. The churches should be turned into stables, and the whole clergy should feel the weight of their vengeance when they returned, as they were sure to do, in triumph. But Ambrose was not terrified by such menaces, and had firm faith in the Providence which he believed to be watching over the orthodox and lawful emperor. No sooner did he hear of their departure than he started for Milan, and arrived there on the 1st of August. Meanwhile, the usurper and his barbarian patron had reached the banks of the Frigidus, a small stream which rises in the Julian Alps, and joins the main stream of the Isonzo at no great distance from Aquileia. Here they awaited the coming of the Eastern emperor. An indecisive skirmish, terminating rather to the disadvantage of Theodosius, revealed the weakness of his barbarian allies and the inferiority of his numbers: the Western commanders were inspired with fresh courage, while the generals on the other side began to despair. They recommended a cessation of hostilities, and advised their master to wait till the next spring, when he might hope to take the field with an increased and adequate force.   But he saw that delay would be certain loss to himself and gain to his opponents, and refused to retire.   The Cross, he said, which was the standard of his army, must needs prevail over the image of Hercules, which was borne in the ranks of the enemy.   Entering a little chapel which stood on the crest of the hill on which his men were encamped, he prostrated himself, and spent the night in prayer. About the time of cock-crow he was overpowered by sleep.   As he slept he thought he saw a vision.   Two men in white garments appeared to him, and announced themselves as the apostles St. John and St. Philip.   They bade him take courage, and engage the enemy boldly, for that they were sent to be with him and give him aid.   This promise tallied with a prophecy he had received before his march, from his old friend, the ascetic John of Egypt, who predicted that he would gain the victory, but with severe loss.   Awaking from his slumber, he finished his prayer, and then, encouraging his men by an account of his dream, led them on to battle, or, as his opponents thought, to certain destruction.   It was a bold step, certainly, for Arbogastes had during the night sent a body of troops to take him in the rear, and they could already be seen occupying the passes that lay behind him.   His mind, however, was soon set at rest by a message from the commanders of these troops.   Had they been friendly to their original leader, Theodosius

would, in all human probability, have been, before the
close of the day, a fugitive or a prisoner; but they
were disgusted with the Frank and his creature,
their master, and distrustful of their success or of
their skill, and were ready to desert them and
join the rival emperor. Besides these unhoped-
for allies, Theodosius was favoured by the weather.
It was the 7th of September, and the ground was
covered with dust, which a brisk wind at his back
blew into the face of the enemy, at the same time
retarding the flight of their spears and arrows, and increasing the velocity of those which were launched
against them. A slight appearance of reluctance
which presented itself in one place was dispelled by
the promptitude and zeal of the Eastern commander.
Leaping from his horse, he put himself at the head
of the loiterers, and cried, "Where is the God of
Theodosius?" It need hardly be said that the
victory was decisive.

The miserable Eugenius was dragged by a party of his
own men and hurled in fetters at the feet of the conqueror. He pleaded for mercy, but in vain; the soldiers
were not likely to listen to such an appeal, and Theodosius himself could not but remember Valentinian.
Personally, the poor wretch was beneath contempt,
but he wore the purple, and had been saluted emperor; it was not safe to spare him. Arbogastes fled,
and wandered for some days among the mountains,
desolate and desperate. But escape was hopeless,
and the high-spirited Frank, rather than fall into the
power of the victor, and die an ignominious death, or
sue for a yet more ignominious life, decided the
matter for himself with the point of his own sword.

Ambrose was made aware of the victory by a letter from the emperor, which called upon him to render special thanks to God for His merciful preservation of the empire and His care of its ruler. The letter contained a gentle hint that the bishop's protracted absence from Milan looked as if he had begun to lose faith in the writer's cause, or to fancy that he was no longer an object of Divine favour and under the protection of Providence. Ambrose hastened to disavow such a feeling, and to assure the emperor of the real cause of his absence. He congratulated him heartily on his success, and commended his pious humility in the midst of triumph. "I took your Piety's letter with me," he wrote, "and laid it on the altar, and held it in my hand when I made the oblation." Finally, he reminded him of the duty of being merciful. There was every reason why he should refer to this subject. A large number of persons, most of them more or less compromised by adherence to Eugenius, but some few of them guiltless of any but compulsory submission to him, had taken refuge in the churches. Ambrose knew, by experience, what Theodosius's temper was, and what direction the counsel of his advisers was likely to take, and dreaded both that the sanctity of churches might be invaded, and that severity might be used towards men who might be won by clemency, or, indeed, towards those who had rather deserved encouragement and consolation. He, therefore, not only mentioned their case in writing, but instructed Felix, his deacon (afterwards Bishop of Bologna), who was the bearer of the letter, to plead for them. Not long after, he wrote again to intercede on behalf of these wretched fugitives, mercy to whom would be a fit thank-offering for victory. " Their tears," he said, " I cannot endure without sending a supplication to forestall your Clemency's coming." The emperor responded to his appeal by despatching an officer to take charge of the suppliants; and Ambrose thought it best not to trust to letters, but to have a personal interview. He went to Aquileia, and was received with every mark of respect and affection. The emperor granted his requests ; he knew, he said, how much he owed to the prayers of Ambrose ; he felt also, doubtless, that to be merciful was to be wise. The event did not disappoint him : the pardoned adherents of Eugenius were among the most faithful to him and to his sons.

Theodosius was on the point of starting for Milan, but Ambrose returned with all possible speed, and was fortunate enough to be in the city in time to receive him with those honours which he was glad to see bestowed, not so much on a triumphant soldier as on a God-fearing prince. There was in truth every cause for rejoicing. Once more there was a gleam of hope for mourning Italy, a glimpse of peace for the distracted empire ; once more East and West were united—though for the last time—under a single and a capable head.

It was not to last long. The anxieties of rule, and the fatigues and perils of the late campaign had told upon Theodosius. But a few weeks had elapsed from the date of his victory at the Frigidus, when he was taken ill of dropsy. The unusual inclemency of the weather, excessive rain and dense fog having prevailed for many days, perhaps aggravated his disease ; at all events, he became convinced before very long that his end was near. He had left Arcadius, the elder of his sons, in charge of the East, and now sent for the younger, Honorius, whom he intended to place on the Western throne. The young Cæsar reached his destination safely, and the satisfaction of seeing him and his elder brother, who accompanied him, caused the Imperial sufferer to rally for a short time; so that Arcadius felt justified in returning forthwith to the Eastern capital, where his presence was needed. A splendid show of horse and chariot races in the Circus (a favourite exhibition at Milan, as indeed at all Italian cities), in honour of the prince's arrival, was fixed for January 16th, 395. The emperor attended the morning's show, took interest in the proceedings, and seemed to all to be in improved health. But appearances were delusive. After the midday meal the more aggravated symptoms of his malady began to show themselves; the exertion had probably been too much for him. He was unable to appear again at the races, and Honorius was compelled to attend alone and represent him. He grew rapidly worse, and in the course of the night passed away from the troubles of his high dignity to rejoin his beloved Flaccilla in another world. In his last moments he commended his young sons to the care of the great Stilicho, husband of his niece Serena; then called for Ambrose, entreated him to be a father to them, as he had been to Gratian and Valentinian, and told him how very near to his heart was the welfare of the Church of Christ.

It was determined that his body should not be

interred at Milan, but should be conveyed to Constantinople, there to lie with the remains of his predecessors in the Empire of the East. Before its
departure, and forty days after his death, solemn
obsequies were celebrated at the city where he had
sinned the great sin of his life, where he had shown
his deep penitence, where he had celebrated his last
triumph, and drawn his last breath. The funeral
oration could be spoken by none but Ambrose. The
rhetorical element, though present and palpable, is
not so painfully prominent in it as in that on the
death of Valentinian. The preacher spoke feelingly
of the ability, clemency, and many virtues of the
departed emperor, paying a compliment to the talents
of his sons and successors which a few years unhappily showed to be entirely undeserved. Most of
all, however, he extolled his humble piety. "No
doubt," he said, "the devout emperor is now at rest,
in peace and light, in the company of the saints who
have gone before." An allusion to Constantine the
Great here led him to digress into an apparently
purposeless narration of the story—or rather the
strange legend—of the finding of the Cross by Helena.
Finally, he comforted poor little Honorius, who sat
crying bitterly at not being allowed to accompany his
father's body and go back to his brother Arcadius at
Constantinople, his old home. The preacher reminded
him that he was now an emperor, and had a solemn
duty towards all, so that he must no longer think of
his father only. "Do not fear," he concluded, "that
your father's triumphant remains, wherever they may
go, will appear shorn of honour. Italy does not

think so, she who has beheld magnificent triumphs, and whose children, freed a second time from tyrants, are waiting to extol the author of their liberty. Constantinople does not think so, who sent forth her prince a second time to victory, and, much as she would, could not retain him. She looked for triumphal solemnities on his return, to do honour to his victories; she looked for an emperor of the whole world, surrounded with an army from Gaul, supported by the forces of the whole world. But Theodosius now returns to her with higher power, with greater glory, for it is a troop of angels that accompanies him, a crowd of saints that follows him. Blessed indeed is the city that is receiving an inhabitant of Paradise, and will entertain, in the splendid abode where his body is to rest, a denizen of the heavenly city above."

CHAPTER XV.

THE END OF A GREAT LIFE.

A.D. 395–397.

AMBROSE'S own term was now drawing to a close. He was in his fifty-fifth year, scarcely more than a middle-aged man according to our reckoning. But the anxieties and labours of twenty years had had their effect upon him ; and his ascetic mode of life, if it enhanced his spiritual powers, did not certainly increase his physical strength. He allowed himself no midday meal except on Sundays and saints' days, and, owing to a fortunate peculiarity of his own church, on Saturdays also ; the Saturday feast, we learn, was one of the usages of the Church of Milan, for in Rome the " Sabbath " (the day before the Lord's Day) was kept as a fast. And at the same time he was continually engaged in preaching, writing (not by an amanuensis, but with his own hand), and in giving counsel to those who resorted to him. The wear of this branch of the pastoral office must have been excessive. Numbers flocked to him to give him their confidences before performing that public penance for sin which was customary at that time, and to ask his advice and consolation ; and he threw himself heart and soul into each case, "rejoicing," says Paulinus, "with them that did rejoice, and weeping with them that did weep; for he would weep so with one who acknowledged his errors with a view to penance, as to force him to weep also." His assiduity about the due performance of the rites of religion was equally great, and involved almost an equal tax on his energies, for he would do single-handed at baptisms what five bishops of his time could scarcely perform together. When we remember that at Milan in the fourth century "a baptism" implied commonly the immersion of a number of adults, and was not confined to the pouring of water on a few infants, we shall see that the bodily fatigue of a solemn baptismal day to the officiating bishop (for it was he, not the presbyters, still less the deacons, who usually administered the sacrament) must have been enormous.

The death of Theodosius, while it could have no effect upon his austerities and his labours, must have increased tenfold his anxieties for Church and State. The Huns, a new and terrible enemy, were beginning to threaten the East. The Goths, under Alaric, were stirring in Greece. Gildo the Moor (the brother of that Firmus whom the father of Theodosius had subdued for Valentinian I. in 374) was a rebel, and all but independent, in Africa, and had proclaimed himself a supporter of the persecuting Donatists. With a gentle but unpromising boy of ten (Honorius) for emperor of the West, and an equally gentle fool of eighteen (Arcadius) ruling in the East, guided by the contemptible and irreligious Rufinus, the most dismal forebodings

respecting the Empire were inevitable. But the battle
of the Faith was already won in the West, and no one
had contributed more to the victory than the great
Bishop of Milan himself. That man could not fail to
leave his mark upon the Church who had brought a
Theodosius to do penance and converted an Augustine. Three years later (398), John, the eloquent
and fearless preacher of Antioch, was to ascend the
patriarchal throne of Constantinople, and leave his
mark too behind him, as a champion of the truth in
the East, following up and completing the work of
Basil and Gregory Nazianzen. The Church was sure
to hold her own when it pleased her Divine Master to
send her such rulers as Ambrose and Chrysostom.

Stilicho, who was during the minority of Honorius
the virtual Emperor of the West, and had taken
care to prevent, by the death of Rufinus, the presence of a rival in the East, discovered soon that
the old spirit was not extinct in the Bishop of Milan.
One Cresconius, a criminal, had been condemned to
be exposed to the wild beasts in the Amphitheatre.
Christianity had not yet succeeded in inducing the
Romans to lay aside their barbarous delight in the
sanguinary spectacles of the arena ; it has not yet led
their Spanish descendants to give up the bull-fight,
and only a century ago similar "sports" were not
unknown to the inhabitants of a western isle who
prided themselves on possessing a purer form of
Christianity than that of modern Spain, or, as some of
them even said, than that of Milan fourteen centuries
before. The unhappy wretch had managed to make
his escape, and fled for refuge into a church. Stilicho

was persuaded to order a detachment of soldiers to drag him from the sanctuary. Disregarding the protests and the resistance of the bishop and his clergy, a body of men, headed, said the Catholic gossip of the day, by some Arian officers (probably Goths), forced their way into the sacred building and tore the miserable Cresconius away.

The privilege of sanctuary would be justly considered by nations like ourselves, with a settled constitutional government and a regular judicial system, to be a meaningless and intolerable interference with the due course of the law ; it was by no means without its use at other times and among other people. It often afforded a means of appeal against an unjust or too rigorous sentence, against the passion of a despot, or the baseness of a mercenary judge. It would nowadays be a dangerous advantage to the guilty ; it was once a shield to the innocent. Guilty therefore as the man was, and little as Ambrose desired to infringe on the majesty of the law or thwart its action, he felt deeply moved at this desecration of his church by the violent encroachment on its recognized privilege. It was in his sight an insult to Him to Whom the place was dedicated, and implied a disregard of its sanctity which might eventually terminate in such buildings being handed over for Arian worship, or secular or even heathen purposes. Throwing himself on his knees before the altar, he prayed with many sighs and tears. Stilicho, meanwhile, had begun to regret (we may believe for religious as well as political reasons) the order he had given, and the intelligence brought to him of the conduct of the bishop and clergy increased the feeling. It chanced that the soldiers who had been foremost in the proceedings at the church contrived, in some manner or other, to get into the way of some African leopards which had been let into the arena to do their murderous work, and the beasts, not being able to distinguish between criminals and executioners, had attacked and severely wounded them. This occurrence, in which some imagined that they saw the interposition of a Higher Power, may possibly have influenced Stilicho still further; it certainly did not prejudice the people against his decision, which was that the criminal's life should be spared, and his sentence commuted to exile. The Christians could overlook the arrest of a malefactor within the walls of a church, provided such arrest did not lead to the shedding of blood.

It was about the same time that Ambrose received a deputation from a new convert to Christianity, Fritigil, queen of the Marcomanni, a German tribe inhabiting part of the modern Bohemia, and in past times, with their allies the Sarmatian Quadi, a terrible disquiet to the Roman Empire. The missionary who won Fritigil to the faith had told her much of the greatness of the Milanese prelate, to whom she accordingly sent, entreating him to give her further instruction. He replied by writing, and placing in the hands of her messenger, a catechism, which she gladly received. It has unfortunately been lost. He did not forget the statesman; with his religious instruction he joined a recommendation, which she acted upon, to persuade her husband to make peace, and join in alliance with Rome.

We find Ambrose in the same year (396) not only seconding missionary endeavours, but also called upon to remember his duty as archbishop. The bishopric of Vercelli had become vacant by the death of Limenius, and there was so much strife and party feeling that no election could be made, and the see had remained for some time unfilled. The metropolitan was held responsible for this state of things, either because he had thrown difficulties in the way, or because he had neglected to take the necessary steps towards reconciling the differences and procuring an election. In either case the charge against him was unfair, and without real grounds. In self-defence, and in discharge of his archiepiscopal duty, he addressed a long letter to the Church of Vercelli. It is the last of his which we possess. He urges Churchmen to lay their strife aside, and be at peace, as though Christ Himself were standing among them ; and then cautions them against Sarmatio and Barbatianus, two monks whom he had ejected from his monastery in 391 for teaching some of the doctrines of Jovinian. Next he gives a sketch, illustrated from Scripture, of the qualities needed in their bishop, who ought to combine the virtues of the clerical and monastic life; and winds up with some holy counsel to the laity : the rich, the young, the married, masters, and servants, have their special precepts in this fatherly exhortation. The episcopal election was soon made ; the choice of the Church fell upon Honoratus, who was consecrated as Limenius's successor.

It was not long after writing this letter,—sometime

in February, 397,—that he was called upon to officiate at the consecration of the Bishop of Pavia. After returning from the service he was taken ill, and compelled to retire to his bed. It was soon only too evident to all that his danger was extreme. Stilicho, who had learnt his worth from Theodosius and from his own experience, felt that his loss would be a terrible blow to Italy. Something must be done, he thought, to bring it about that so valuable a life might be spared. Summoning all the most influential and valued of the bishop's friends, he by turns entreated and commanded them to go to his bedside and bid him pray to be permitted to live. They went and proffered their strange request : the dying prelate calmly replied, "I have not so lived among you as to be ashamed to live on : but I do not fear to die, for our Lord is good." The prayers, if offered, were in God's providence not granted : the end drew visibly nearer, and men began to think who should be chosen to fill his place when he was taken from them. It happened that four deacons (one of whom, Venerius, afterwards became Bishop of Milan himself) were standing at the farther end of the gallery in which his couch was placed, and conversing, as they thought, in a scarcely audible tone on this important question. But either they forgot, in their warmth, to moderate their voices, or the sick man's senses, as not unfrequently happens, were preternaturally sharpened : when they mentioned the name of Simplician, they were terrified to hear the bishop express his approval by exclaiming three times, "Old, but good." It is perhaps unnecessary to add that Simplician was his successor.

He sank rapidly; but as the outward man perished,
the inward man was renewed : the Lord Jesus, he told
Bassianus, bishop of Lodi, who had been praying
with him, had come to his side and smiled upon him.
At last (it was Good Friday, April 3, 397) he ceased
to speak : he lay for some hours with his arms
stretched out in the form of the Cross, his lips moving,
but no sound audible.   Midnight passed, and Honoratus the newly-consecrated bishop of Vercelli, who
had been with him, had left his side, and was retiring
to rest, when he thought he heard a voice which
repeated thrice, "Up, hasten, he is departing."
Without delay Honoratus entered the sick chamber,
and gave the dying prelate the Blessed Sacrament of
the Lord's Body and Blood.   He received it, and a
moment after was at rest.   It was Easter Eve, April
4, and his body was carried to the "greater" church :
thence on Easter Day to the church which bears his
name.   There he was laid, close to his beloved brother
Satyrus.   His funeral was attended by a throng of
all ranks and ages : and not Christians only, but
Jews and heathen, came to testify their respect
for the great and holy man who had departed from
among them.   His catechumen Fritigil journeyed all
the way from her German home to see and speak
with him : but she came too late ; she could only
gaze weeping on his honoured tomb.

CHAPTER XVI.

AMBROSE AS POET AND MUSICIAN.

UPWARDS of eighty metrical compositions have been ascribed to the pen of St. Ambrose. The great majority of these are certainly the production of different hands, and of a somewhat later age. There are but twelve which are considered to be indubitably the composition of the great Bishop of Milan, and two of these are found imbedded in liturgical hymns of greater length. He seems, however, to have struck a key-note of Church poetry. "I grant," says Grimm, "that the hymns attributed to Ambrose, whom we may justly call the father of Church song, are not all his; I cannot, however, think that the hymns commonly ascribed to him, but not recognised by editorial critics, were composed later than a century or two after him, they have so much of the simplicity of the others." His metre is for the most part carefully regulated by quantity, though in one or two instances he seems to have neglected quantity for accent, so as to render it necessary for those who recast the hymns of the Roman Breviary in a strictly classical form to make a few alterations. His lines occasionally rhyme, but so irregularly as to make it pretty clear that the rhyme was unintentional. There is no trace of the accentuated metre, with set and perfect rhyme, of the later Latin hymns.

His style as a hymn-writer is throughout grave and severe, but devout, and profoundly accurate in theological expression. More austere than his contemporary Prudentius, and without any of the impassioned fervour of such writers at St. Bernard, he yet impresses us by his dignified simplicity. "We feel," says Archbishop Trench, "as though there were a certain coldness in his hymns, an *aloofness* of the author from his subject, a refusal to blend and fuse himself with it. Only after a while does one learn to feel the grandeur of his unadorned metre, and the profound, though it may have been more instinctive than conscious, wisdom of the poet in choosing it, or to appreciate that noble confidence in the surpassing interest of his theme which has rendered him indifferent to any but its simplest setting forth. It is as though, building an altar to the living God, he would observe the Levitical precept, and rear it of unhewn stones, upon which no tool had been lifted. The great objects of faith in their simplest expression are felt by him so sufficient to stir all the deepest affections of the heart, that any attempt to dress them up, to array them in moving language, were merely superfluous. The passion is there, but it is latent and repressed, a fire burning inwardly, the glow of an austere enthusiasm, which reveals itself, indeed, but not to every careless beholder. Nor do we presently fail to observe how truly these poems belonged to their time, and to the circumstances under which they were produced : how suitably the faith which was in actual conflict with, and was triumphing over, the powers of this world, found its utterance in hymns such as these, wherein is no softness, perhaps little tenderness, but a rock-like firmness, the old Roman stoicism transmuted and glorified into that nobler Christian courage, which encountered and at length overcame the world."

The grandest and noblest of his hymns, in the opinion of all editors, is that for Advent. An almost literal rendering of a portion of it may serve to give an idea of its stern simplicity. The metre employed, the rhymeless eight-syllable line, is that of the original.

> Redeemer of the nations, come,
> Show them a virgin mother's Child :
> Amazed be all the wondering world,
> For such a birth beseems our God.
>
> *   *   *   *
>
> " Out of His chamber" He proceeds,
> That royal hall of purity,
> " A giant," [1] of two natures joined,
> " To run His course " rejoicingly.
>
> He goeth from the Father forth,
> And to the Father speeds again,
> Descending to the deep of hell,
> Returning to the throne of God.
>
> With the Eternal Father One,
> With belt of flesh Thou girdest Thee,
> The weakness of our mortal frame
> So strengthening with enduring might.

---

[1] The "giants" of Gen. vi. 4 were considered to be creatures of a double nature, the offspring of women wedded to spiritual beings ; or, as the mythology of Hesiod has it, of Ouranos (heaven), and Ge (earth). The term "giant" is applied in Ps. xix. 5 to the Sun of Righteousness : and this was imagined to be because of His two natures, Human and Divine. It may be as well to add that the Hebrew words rendered "giant" in the two passages are quite different.

Now brightly shines Thy manger-bed,
And night a new-born radiance breathes,
Which nightly shade shall never dim,
Which shines to faith eternally.

There is much severe beauty in the Matin Hymn.
The version given imitates its occasional rhyme.

O Partner of the Father's light,
Thyself the Light of Light, and Day,
With hymns we bring to end the night :
Be with us as we kneel and pray.

Remove the darkness of our minds,
And chase the demon troops away ;
Banished be slothfulness by Thee,
Lest it o'erwhelm the idle soul.

So, Christ, have mercy on us all,
Who all believe and hope in Thee :
Blest to thy suppliant servants be
This early strain of holy psalm.

The contribution of Ambrose to the music of the
Western Church has been so thoroughly remodelled
and systematized by St. Gregory, that it is impossible
to determine exactly what and how much is due to
the master-mind of Milan. It seems clear[1] that he
introduced the practice of antiphonal chanting from
the East, and probably not a few of the melodies he
employed were from the same source. Some have
imagined that these melodies were a reproduction of
those used in the Temple service at Jerusalem, tradi-
tionally preserved both by Jews and Christians in the
churches and synagogues of the East, and that the

[1] See p. 57.

Ambrosian basilica, while the faithful kept their vigils within its walls, resounded to strains in which David and Solomon had joined some fourteen centuries before. But our ignorance of the Hebrew gamut, and the probability that it differed essentially from the four Greek scales with which Ambrose was acquainted, renders this opinion less tenable than beautiful. It would certainly seem to link us yet more closely with the chosen people under the older covenant if we could think that not our psalter only, but our chant also, was an inheritance from the sweet psalmists of Israel; but fact refuses to give way to sentiment.

Compared with the popular church music of our own time, the Ambrosian music appears as severe as the Ambrosian poetry. And yet, as the latter was a comfort to St. Augustine when he lay awake and thought sadly yet joyfully of his departed mother, so the music touched his heart when first he joined in it as a Christian. "How I wept," he says, "at Thy hymns and canticles, touched to the quick by the voices of Thy melodious Church! Those voices flowed into my ears, and the truth distilled into my heart, and thence there streamed forth a devout emotion, and my tears ran down, and it was well with me therein." And though he elsewhere says he dreaded lest he should give too much attention to the sound, too little to the sense, and was disposed to banish all chanting from the churches, save the simple "plain tune, after the manner of distinct reading," used in Alexandria by the command of St. Athanasius, he cannot help admitting the value of the Church's song, and, by implication, commending the work of

St. Ambrose in connexion with it. "When I remember the tears I shed at the chants of Thy Church when first I recovered my faith, and that I am moved not by the chant, but by what is chanted, when it is chanted with a clear voice and suitable modulation, I acknowledge again the great usefulness of the institution."

CHAPTER XVII.

ST. AMBROSE AS A THEOLOGIAN.

IT is one of the marvels which meet us in the course
of ecclesiastical history, that Ambrose, the lawyer and
unbaptized layman, became in a week the profoundly
learned and devoted prelate.[1]   Though not yet baptized, he had been early admitted a catechumen,
and no doubt had been allowed access to the Holy
Scriptures and to the writings of Christian authors,
both of his own and of earlier times.   And of this
access he must have availed himself largely.   Within
a few months from his baptism he writes a work, that
on Paradise, full of scriptural allusions and deep
divinity.   That much of his theology is borrowed is
true : that is to say, we recognise in his writings that
he has been consulting the works of others ; and we
know as a fact that he was a good Greek scholar, and
a student of Philo, Origen, and Basil.   But his depth
and accuracy are all his own.   He writes as one who has
read and thought too.   The promising young advocate,
the busy lawyer and politician, the elegant scholar,
had not confined his studies to the things of this
world.   Side by side with his Cicero and his Virgil,

[1] See pp. 28, 29.

his Æschylus and his Plato, had been well-used rolls, treating of higher matters than philosophy or law or romance,—the eternal truths revealed by the Eternal Spirit. And his spirit had communed with them. The same God who in His providence had designed to call him from the council-chamber to the altar had in the same providence guided his mind not to things temporal only, but to things eternal : so that when the call came, the chosen vessel was not unprepared for the Master's use. His legal training was not without its happy effect : it moulded him into that accuracy of thought and expression which is so remarkable in all his writings. He does not, how-ever, approve, as a rule, of teaching Christian mysteries to the unbaptized. The doctrine of the sacraments, if communicated before baptism to the uninitiated, would, he thought, damage rather than edify.

We, in our Western Church, and in this nineteenth century, are more interested than we are generally aware in his theology and his theological method. We are so accustomed to connect the great name of Athanasius with that cardinal doctrine, the coequal Deity of the Redeemer and the Sanctifier, that we suffer its brilliancy to overpower the brightness of the other scarcely less illustrious champions of the truth as it is in Jesus. Yet it is the fact that the West owes a vast debt to Ambrose. It was he more, perhaps, than any other Western father, whose energy and theological definiteness checked the wave of Arianism which the semi-Christian Goths were bringing with them, and which, but for him, would have spread over Italy, Spain, Gaul, and Britain. Not in the synod of Aquileia only, but in almost every writing that has come down to us from his pen, as in almost every one of his public acts, we find him the devoted defender of the Nicene teaching, that the Son is consubstantial with the Father.   But there is more than this.   Of all the Fathers, from St. Ignatius down to St. Bernard, none exerted such an influence over the Latin Church as St. Augustine of Hippo. He is, without the possibility of gainsaying it, the leading spirit of Western theology : "no sermon with-out Augustine" is a Spanish proverb ; and we all remember our own Chaucer's

> " But I ne cannot boult it to the bren,
>   As can the holy Doctour Seynt Austen."

And not only so, but he was in an especial manner the favourite of the chiefs of the Reformation.   The same fatalist tendency which, we would almost say, inevitably characterized Augustine as a converted Manichæan, the adversary of Pelagius, made him dear to those who were lifting up their voices against the will-worship and the Pelagian self-righteousness which connected themselves with the teaching of Rome.   To those who felt and knew that " the way of man is not in himself" even the horrors of " reprobation " seemed nearer the truth than the idea of deserving grace of congruity, or accumulating merit by ascetic self-inaceration, or profuse and inconsiderate almsgiving. On the other hand, we can hardly help seeing that the same Augustinian theosophy, coarsely stated and unduly pressed, has exercised an unhappy influence on our own times by being, to some extent at least, the source of no small portion of the infidelity of these later days. Men have shrunk from belief in the God of revelation, because He was represented to them as One who deliberately created with the purpose of consigning His creatures helplessly and hopelessly to never-ending misery.

If then Augustine has so influenced for Western Christians the middle ages, the Reformation, and the nineteenth century, we cannot but be deeply interested in one who had so much to do as Ambrose with forming and directing the Christianity of Augustine. For though in some points the scholar may have broken away from the master, or modified his teaching, still we must in the main be feeling the results of Ambrose's mode of dealing with his noble convert. We cannot tell to what extent his calm judgment may have negatively influenced that convert, and preserved him from carrying to an erroneous extreme those principles on which others have framed a mistaken, not to say repulsive, system of divinity. If Augustine is what he is with the teaching of Ambrose, what might he have been without that teaching? The bishop of Milan was at least the guide of the guide of the theology of the West.

The writings of Ambrose all abound with definite theology; but the distinctly dogmatic treatises which we have from his pen are those on the Faith, in five books, on the Holy Ghost, in three books, on the Incarnation, and on the Mysteries.

The history of the five books on the Faith (A.D. 378–9) has already been told. They are directed, he informs us in the outset of the first book, mainly against the errors of Sabellius, Photinus, and Arius ; and he briefly confutes all three from the opening verses of St. John's gospel (i. § 56).

"*In the beginning was the Word, and the Word was with God, and the Word was God. The same was in the beginning with God.*' 'Was with God' he says, and repeats ' was ' four times. Where does the scoffer find that He was not ? Elsewhere, too, St. John in his Epistle says, *That which was in the beginning*: 'was' has an indefinite extent; whatever explanation you may devise, the Son 'was.' Our fisherman has in this short paragraph excluded all heresies. 'That which was in the beginning' is not included in time nor preceded by a beginning. So Arius may hold his tongue. And that which 'was with God' is not confused by mixture, but kept distinct by the solid perfection of the Word which remains with the Father ; so that Sabellius may be silent. *And the Word was God.* Therefore this Word is not in the utterance of speech, but in the designation of heavenly power, so that Photinus is confuted. And as He 'was in the beginning with God,' the inseparable unity of the Eternal Divinity in the Father and the Son is plainly taught, so that Eunomius[1] is put to the blush."

And again (v. § 104) : "*If David then in spirit call Him Lord, how is He his son ?* By one question our Lord has shut out the Sabellians, the Photinians,

[1] Eunomius was a disciple of Aetius, who taught that the Son was unlike (*anomoios*) in nature to the Father ; whence the name of Anomoians given to his party. Eunomius was made Bishop of Cyzicus about A.D. 360, but was soon afterwards deposed for heresy.

and the Arians.   For when it says *The Lord said to my Lord*, Sabellius is shut out, who will have it that the Father is the same as the Son; Photinus, who judges according to the flesh, is shut out, because none could be Lord of King David but One who is God, for it is written, *Thou shalt worship the Lord thy God, and Him only shalt thou serve*. Would a prophet reigning under the Law hold an opinion contrary to the Law?   Arius is shut out, who hears that the Son 'sits at the right hand' of the Father; so that if he argues from human usage, he convicts himself, and pours back on himself the poison of his sacrilegious argument, and, while he interprets the inequality of Father and Son after human fashion, erring from the truth in respect of Both, advances the One Whose honour he seeks to diminish, being ready to own Him to be first Whom he hears to be on the right hand. The Manichæan is shut out also; for He does not deny Himself to be Son of David according to the flesh, since when the blind men cried, *Jesus, thou Son of David, have mercy on us*, He was pleased with their faith, and stopped and healed them; but He declares that it does not agree with His proper eternity that He should be named by the faithless 'son of David' only.   For He is Son of God against Ebion, Son of David against the Manichæans; Son of God against Photinus, Son of David against Marcion; Son of God against Paul of Samosata, Son of David against Valentinus; Son of God against Arius and Sabellius, inheritors of pagan error, Lord of David against the Jews, who, when they saw the Son of God in the flesh, with unholy madness believed Him to be a mere man.

But in the Church's faith the Son of God the Father and the Son of David is one and the same; because the mystery of the incarnation of God is the salvation of the whole creation, as it is written that He *by the grace*[1] *of God should taste death for every man;* that is, that, without any suffering on the part of His Divinity, the whole creation should be redeemed by the price of the Lord's blood; as it runs in another place, *the creature shall be delivered from the bondage of corruption.* It is, therefore, one thing to be called Son with reference to the Divine Substance, another to be so called with reference to the taking flesh upon Him : for in respect of the Divine generation the Son is equal to God the Father, and in respect of His taking flesh He is a servant; for *He took on Him,* says the Apostle, *the form of a servant;* but still the Son is one and the same. On the other hand, in respect of His glory He is Lord of the holy patriarch David; according to the sequence of corporeal succession He is His son, not as coming short of Himself, but as gaining for Himself the right of our adoption."

All passages of Scripture which seem to speak of the Son as inferior to the Father are to be referred, he shows, to Christ's humanity (ii. § 59) : " It was in His human nature that He doubted, and was weary, and rose again, for it is that which has fallen that rises. In His human nature, too, He said that on

---

[1] St. Ambrose here reads " without " God instead of " by the grace " of God. Theodoret and Theophylact do the same, alleging that the ordinary reading is Nestorian, separating the Manhood from the Godhead of Jesus Christ. St. Ambrose understands it of the impassibility of the Divine Nature.

which a question is often raised, *My Father is greater than I.* . . . He is less than the Father in His human nature ; can you wonder if He, speaking in the person of a man, called the Father greater, when in the person of a man He said *I am a worm and no man,* and again *He was brought as a sheep to the slaughter ?* If in this respect you call Him ' less,' I cannot deny it ; but, to use the language of Scripture, He was not born less, but 'made lower.' Why made lower? *Being in the form of God, He thought it not robbery to be equal with God, but made Himself of no reputation ;* not, certainly, relinquishing what He had, but assuming what He had not, for *He took on Him the form of a servant.* In short, that we might know that He was made lower by taking a body on Him, David showed that he was prophesying of a man, by saying *What is man that Thou art mindful of him, or the Son of man that Thou visitest him ? Thou hast made Him a little lower than the angels.* And the apostle, interpreting this passage, says : *We see Jesus, Who was made a little lower than the angels, for the suffering of death crowned with glory and honour, that He without God*[1] *should taste death for every man.* . . . How well the apostle has put it, *without God should taste death for every man,* lest we should imagine that the suffering was of His divinity, not of his flesh! "

Again, referring to a text continually alleged by the Arians, he remarks : " Hence we understand that what was written of the Incarnation of the Lord, *The Lord created me the beginning of His ways, for His*

---

[1] See preceding note.

works,[1] signifies that the Lord Jesus was created of a virgin to redeem the works of the Father.   It cannot be doubted that this was said of the mystery of the Incarnation, since the Lord took flesh to free His works from the bondage of corruption, and to destroy, by the suffering of His own Body, him who had the power of death.   For the flesh of Christ was for the sake of the works, His Divinity before the works : because *He is before all things, and by Him all things consist.*"

It would be wrong to omit the powerful logic by which he substantiates that article of the Athanasian creed, " the Son uncreate " (v. § 137).

" The Son is the Lord of Glory (for the apostle speaks of ' crucifying the Lord of Glory') ; but glory is not given to creatures ; therefore the Son is not a creature.

" The Son is the ' express image' of the Father. Now every creature is unlike heavenly existence ; but the Son is not unlike God the Father ; therefore the Son is not a creature.

" The Son *thought it not robbery to be equal with God.* Now no creature is equal with God, but the Son is equal ; therefore the Son is not a creature.

" Every creature is changeable ; but the Son of God is not changeable ; therefore the Son of God is not a creature.

[1] Prov. viii. 22.   The passage in the Hebrew was as it is rendered in the Latin Vulgate and our Authorized Version, "The Lord possessed me in the beginning of His way, before His works of old."   But in the LXX., which St. Ambrose's version follows, an itacism pointed out by St. Jerome has turned " possessed " into " created."

"Every creature, by its own natural capacity, receives the accidents both of good and of evil, and perceives the abatement of them; but with the Son of God there can be no addition to or abatement of His Divinity; therefore the Son of God is not a creature.

"God will *bring every work* of His *into judgment;* but the Son of God is not brought into judgment, for He Himself is Judge; therefore the Son of God is not a creature.

". . . . The Son quickens, as the Father; *for as the Father raiseth up the dead and quickeneth them, even so the Son quickeneth whom He will;* the Son raises as the Father does, the Son preserves as the Father does; how can He be unequal in power Who is not unequal in grace? So also the Son, as the Father, does not destroy. Therefore, that no one should fancy there were two Gods, or introduce a division of power, He said *I and My Father are One.* How can a creature say this? Therefore the Son of God is not a creature.

" To be a king and to be a slave are not the same thing. Now Christ is a king, and the son of a king; therefore the Son of God is not a slave. But every creature is a slave, whereas the Son of God, who from slaves makes sons of God, is no slave; therefore the Son of God is not a creature."

The discourse on the Lord's Incarnation was composed and delivered, A.D. 382, at the request of two Arian courtiers of Gratian. The two gentlemen, after challenging the bishop to handle the subject, were discourteous enough, according to Paulinus, to take a drive out in a gig when they ought to have gone to church to hear his sermon, and suffered for their offence by being thrown from their carriage and killed.

The treatise, as we might expect, traverses much the same ground with the five books on the Faith, and the author confesses as much (ch. vii.). It is necessary for him, however, not only to insist upon the consubstantial Deity, but to maintain against opponents the perfect and sinless Humanity of Christ (§ 59).

"It is written, they say, that *the Word was made flesh.* It is written, I do not deny it ; but consider what follows, *And dwelt among us* [*in us*], that is, the Word who took flesh dwelt in us, dwelt, that is, in human flesh, and therefore was called *Emmanuel,* that is, *God with us.* So *the Word was made flesh* stands for 'was made man.' As also it says in Joel, *I will pour out my Spirit upon all flesh ;* for this does not mean upon irrational flesh, but a coming out-pouring of spiritual grace on men is promised. Suppose you take it literally, and imagine from the expression *the Word was made flesh* that the Word of God was changed into flesh, you cannot deny that it is written of the Lord that *He did no sin,* but *was made sin.* Was the Lord therefore changed into sin? No, but He was called sin because He took our sins on Him. For the Lord was called *a curse,* not because He was changed into a curse, but because He took on Him the curse which belonged to us, for *cursed is every one,* it says, *that hangeth on a tree.* You cannot then wonder that it is written *the Word was made flesh,*

when the flesh was taken up by the Word of God ;
since it is written of the sin which He had not that
He was made sin, that is, not by nature and the
operation of sin, though He was *made in the likeness
of sinful flesh*, but, in order that He might crucify our
sin in His flesh, He took upon Himself for us the
weaknesses of a body already liable to the consequences of fleshly sin."

But the sinless body is not perfect man without a
soul (§§ 63, 68).

"And therefore, when He took man's flesh, it follows
that He took the perfection and fulness of incarnation, for nothing in Christ is imperfect.   Therefore,
He took flesh to raise it again ; He took a soul, but
a perfect, reasonable, human soul. . . . . What use
would it have been to take flesh without soul, since
the flesh is certainly insensible, and the irrational
soul is neither liable to the consequences of sin, nor
worthy of reward ? He therefore took for us that
which in us was still in danger. What use is it to
me if He did not redeem the whole of me ? But He
did redeem the whole of man, who said, *Are ye angry
at Me because I have made a man every whit whole on
the Sabbath day ?* He redeemed the whole of me,
because the believer rises again into a perfect man,
not in part, but wholly."

And this perfect God-man is the revelation of the
Father to men (§ 112).

"The Father then is holy, and the Father is perfect ; the Son too is holy and perfect, as the image
of God.   The image of God, because all that belongs
to God is seen in the Son, namely eternal Divinity,

Omnipotence, and Majesty. As, then, God is, so is
He seen in His image. Whence you must needs
believe the image of God to be such as God is. For
if you withdraw anything from the image, it will surely
appear withdrawn from Him Whose the image is ; if
you believe the image to be deficient, God will appear
in His image less than He really is. For as you
estimate the image, such will that Invisible One, of
Whom the image is, appear to you. The image said,
He that hath seen Me hath seen the Father. And as
you estimate Him whose image you believe the Son
to be, so of necessity must the Son be estimated by
you. Whence, as the Father is uncreate, the Son
also is uncreate ; as the Father is not deficient, the
Son is not deficient ; as the Father is almighty, the
Son is almighty."

The three books on the Holy Ghost were written
at the request of the Emperor Gratian in the year
(A.D. 381) in which the doctrines of Macedonius and
the Pneumatomachi were condemned by the first
Council of Constantinople. Ambrose seems to allude
to the decline of the Arian party in the prologue :
" Even Constantinople," he says, with a slight under-
current of Occidental jealousy, " has now received the
word of God." He culled materials for the work
from Didymus, Basil, his brother Gregory of Nyssa,
Athanasius, and other writers ; and Jerome most
unfairly ridicules him as not having improved his
authors in the process of translation, and as having
produced a poor and weak result, embellished with
rhetorical graces, but wanting in power. A perusal
of the work impresses us with no idea of deficiency

on the part of the writer, but does certainly confirm us in the notion that the critic was not entirely free from prejudice and jealousy. We may admit, however, that the work is not perfection. There is a tendency to repetition, an occasional want of method, and a frequent divergence into mystical interpretations of Scripture very little to the point, which are blemishes in an otherwise great and valuable whole.

The line of argument taken by Ambrose is the simple and logical one that Divine attributes are throughout Scripture given to the Holy Spirit ; that in respect of grace, love, communion, pardon, light, life, creation, operation, counsel, will, He is One with the other two Holy Persons ; that His Personality is as clearly stated as that of the Son ; and that those expressions which seem to convey the idea of Him as a created or inferior being, are also applied to the Son, so that if they do not disprove the Deity of Christ, they cannot be held to throw any doubt on the Deity of the Spirit. And the warning against false teaching is very solemn (i. § 47).

" Consider carefully why the Lord said, *Whosoever speaketh a word against the Son of Man, it shall be forgiven him ; but whosoever speaketh against the Holy Ghost, it shall not be forgiven him, neither in this world, neither in the world to come.* Is there any difference between the offence against the Son and that against the Holy Spirit ? No ; for as the dignity is one, so the injury is one. But if any one, misled by the appearance of the human body [of Christ], thinks less highly than he should do of the flesh of Christ (for we ought not to have low notions of that

Flesh which is the palace of virtue and the fruit of the Virgin), he is in fault, yet is not excluded from pardon, which he may gain by faith. But if any one denies the dignity, majesty, and power of the Holy Ghost to be eternal, and imagines that devils are cast out, not by God's Spirit, but by Beelzebub, there can be no entreaty for pardon where there is the fulness of sacrilege ; because he who has denied the Spirit, has denied the Father and the Son, since the Spirit of God is the same as the Spirit of Christ."

Ambrose does not hesitate to speak of the Holy Ghost "proceeding" from the Father and the Son ; but he refers the "proceed" apparently to the temporal mission of the Spirit (i. § 114).

"The Spirit, then, is not sent as if from a place, nor does He proceed as from a place when He proceeds from the Son ; as the Son Himself, when He says, *I came forth from the Father, and am come into the world*, destroys all opinions which may be formed of movement, as in bodies, from place to place. Similarly, when we read that God is within or without, we do not include God in, or separate Him from, anybody. . . . Wisdom says, *I came out of the mouth of the Most High*, not so as to be out of the Father, but with the Father, because *the Word was with God ;* and not only with the Father, but in the Father ; for He saith, *I am in the Father, and the Father in Me.* But when He goes forth from the Father, He does not retire from a place, or separate Himself as a body from a body ; nor when He is in the Father is He included as a body in a body. And the Holy Ghost, when He proceeds from the Father and the Son, is not separated from Father or Son ; for how can He be separated from the Father who is the Breath of His mouth ? And this is at once a proof of His Eternity, and an expression of the unity of His Divinity."

We find towards the end of the work an energetic protest against Tritheism (iii. § 95).

" According to our judgment that God is One, there is understood one Divinity, and a oneness of Power As we say that God is One, both confessing the Father with a true name of Deity, and not denying the Son, so we do not exclude the Holy Ghost from the unity of Deity: and yet we do not assert, but deny, three Gods, because it is not oneness but division of power that constitutes plurality. For how can the unity of Divinity admit of plurality, when plurality is of number, and the Divine nature does not admit of number ? (§ 106). But you may say, perhaps, 'If I call the Spirit Lord, I shall speak of three Lords.' But when you call the Son Lord, do you either deny the Son or acknowledge two Lords ? Far from it, for the Son Himself said, *Ye cannot serve two lords* [*masters*] : but He did not deny Himself or the Father to be Lord, for He called the Father Lord, as you find it, *I thank Thee, O Father, Lord of heaven and earth ;* and He spoke of Himself as Lord, as we read in the Gospel, *Ye call me Master and Lord, and ye say well, for so I am.* But He did not speak of two Lords ; on the contrary He showed that He did not when He gave the warning, *Ye cannot serve two Lords.* For there are not two Lords where the Lordship is one ; because the Father is in the Son and the Son in the Father, and therefore there is one

K

Lord. . . . So as we do not say there are two Lords when we style both the Father and the Son Lord, so we do not say there are three Lords, when we confess the Spirit to be Lord. . . . So also the Father is holy, the Son holy, and the Spirit holy, but there are not three Holies, because there is one Holy God, one Lord. For there is one true Holiness, as there is one true Divinity."

The one short tractate, "On the Mysteries" is singularly in accordance with the teaching of our Prayer Book as regards the number of the true Evangelical Sacraments. The "mysteries" are not seven, but two. Not only are we glad to find the "two only" of our own Catechism thus upheld by the authority of one of the four great doctors of the West, but a special interest attaches to the work : it is a reproduction of the course of instruction given to the newly-baptized at Easter 387 ; and there is, as we have seen, every reason to believe that Augustine was one of them. They are solemnly reminded of the various details in the ceremony of their admission into the Christian Church; the entrance into the baptistery, the renunciation of the devil, the turning to the east, the descent into the water, the profession of faith in the One coequal Trinity, the unction, the gospel which tells how our Lord washed His disciples' feet, and the chrisom vest. They are taught that the element of the regenerating sacrament was prefigured in the water of the primeval earth over which the Spirit moved ; in the Flood ; in the cloud-covered sea through which the Hebrews passed ; in the water of Marah, sweetened by the mystic wood ; in the Jordan, where Naaman washed and was cleansed; in the pool of Bethesda, stirred by the angel. But the water is nothing in itself: (§ 19) :—

"You have been told not to believe only what you see; lest you should say, 'Is this the great mystery which *eye hath not seen nor ear heard, neither hath it entered into the heart of man to conceive?* I see water, which I used every day to see; can it cleanse me, whereas I often have gone down into it, and have never been cleansed?' Learn from this that water does not cleanse without the Spirit. And so you have read that the three witnesses in Baptism are one, the spirit, and the water, and the blood : because if you remove one of them, the sacrament of baptism does not exist. For what is water without the Cross of Christ? a common element, without any sacramental efficacy. But again, the mystery of regeneration cannot be without water, for *unless a man be born again of water and of the Spirit, he cannot enter into the kingdom of God.* Now even the catechumen believes in the Cross of Christ, for he too is signed with it:[1] but unless he is baptized in the name of the Father and of the Son and of the Holy Ghost, he cannot receive the remission of sins, nor obtain the gift of spiritual grace."

From the font the newly-baptized proceed to the altar, to partake in that holy feast of which David in mystery sang in the 23rd Psalm; prefigured in the

---

[1] The form of admitting a catechumen included the use of the sign of the cross (*see* p. 4). St. Augustine speaks of himself in childhood as having been "signed with the sign of the Lord's Cross, and salted with His salt." (Confes. I. xi.)

gifts of Melchizedek, and the manna in the desert, but far above either as the light is above the shadow, the reality above the figure ; for Christ Himself is there, to be the spiritual food of His people (§ 58) :— "Whence also the Church, seeing the grace to be so great, exhorts her children and her neighbours to hasten together to the sacrament, saying, *Eat, O friends ; drink, yea, drink abundantly, O beloved.* What we eat and drink the Holy Ghost has expressed for you by the Prophet elsewhere, saying, *O taste and see how gracious the Lord is, blessed is the man who trusteth in Him.* Christ is in that Sacrament, because it is the Body of Christ : it is not therefore a bodily but a spiritual food. Whence also the Apostle says of its type, *Our fathers did eat spiritual meat, and drink spiritual drink ;* for the Body of God is a spiritual Body, the Body of Christ is the Body of a Divine Spirit : for Christ is a Spirit, as we read : *The spirit before our face is Christ the Lord* [*A.V., The breath of our nostrils, the anointed of the Lord.*] And in Peter's Epistle we have *Christ suffered for us.* Finally this meat *strengthens* our *heart,* this drink *makes glad the heart of man,* as the Prophet has declared."

Ambrose evidently did not withhold the cup from the laity, for these words are not addressed to priests, and the theory of concomitance, invented to console the laity for losing half their Eucharist, finds no place in his writings. He did not hold the sacrament to be "a bare sign, an untrue figure of a thing absent"; nor yet did he try to explain the mystery by any device such as that of Transubstantiation, but was contented to believe, without discussing or defining, the Real Spiritual Presence.

CHAPTER XVIII.

ST. AMBROSE AS AN INTERPRETER OF SCRIPTURE.

By far the greater part of the works of St. Ambrose consists of expositions of Scripture. All of these appear, like his works of dogmatic theology, to have been intended for delivery in public, either as set discourses, or in the form of instruction given in what the language of our Church and time would call Bible Classes. We constantly meet with allusions to passages in the service of the day, with parenthetical observations and digressions, and with remarks on incidents of the time, natural enough in a speech, but unlikely to be met with in a carefully-arranged treatise or commentary.

Of comments on the text of Scripture we have two : the " Enarrations " on thirteen Psalms, including the 119th, and an Exposition on the Gospel of St. Luke. The other Expositions are exegetical tractates on the events or personages of the Old Testament. The " Hexaëmeron," or account of the six days of Creation, is, of course, a treatise on that work of the Deity as recorded in the 1st chapter of Genesis ; the remainder are on Adam and Eve (or Paradise), Cain and Abel, Noah, Abraham, Isaac, Jacob, Joseph, the blessings of the Patriarchs, Job, David, Elijah, Naboth, Tobit.

Commentators, both Jewish and Christian, agree

with St. Ambrose that of Scriptural exposition there are at least three (if not four) methods. First comes the historical, literal, or critical, expounding the written Word with reference to its immediate meaning, the time at which and the circumstances under which it was written or spoken, and inquiring into its simple literal import. Secondly, we have the practical, moral, or tropological, examining the teaching of the Word, and the rules which it gives for the direction of our life and actions. Thirdly, there is the spiritual, mystical, or anagogical, pointing out the more or less hidden reference which it bears to Christ and His Kingdom, whether in the way of type and figure, or of implied and covert doctrine. It is to this latter method that Ambrose mainly inclines. If we may judge from his interpretations of Scriptural names, and the extraordinary meanings he attaches to the letters of the Hebrew alphabet in his Commentary on the 119th Psalm, he was entirely ignorant of the original language of the Old Testament: but we know he was an excellent Greek scholar; and he adheres to the guidance of Origen, with whose writings he was conversant, and everywhere seeks to unfold, much as he did, the spiritual significance of the passage, event, or character, with which he is dealing.

Other portions of Scripture lend themselves more readily, some to one, some to another of the three methods; but the Psalter, he says, adapts itself to all (Ps. xxxvii. § 1) :—

"All Divine Scripture is either natural, or mystical, or moral. Natural in Genesis, in which is expressed how the heaven, seas, and earth were made, and how this world was formed. Mystical in Leviticus, in which is contained the mystery of the priesthood. Moral in Deuteronomy, in which man's life is shaped according to the precept of the Law.   Whence also Solomon's three books appear to be chosen out of a number : Ecclesiastes out of the natural, Canticles out of the mystical, Proverbs out of the moral.   But since the body of all the Psalms is one, there is no division or distinction in them, but none of these methods of teaching, whichever the case may require, is omitted from them."

But of the excellence of the spiritual over the other kinds of interpretation he speaks most strongly, comparing the moral and mystical modes to the two sisters of Bethany, and exalting the spiritual Mary far above the practical Martha (Ps. i. ver. 3, § 42).

"The mystical saves and delivers from death : the moral is an ornament for decoration, not a help to our redemption.   That the mystical is more excellent than the moral even our Lord Himself teaches in His Gospel, saying of Mary, who sat at the Lord's feet and heard His word, when Martha was busied about serving, and complained that her own sister did not help her in the duties of the table, *Martha, Martha, Mary hath chosen that good part which shall not be taken away from her.*   If she who waited on Christ at table was not comparable to her who desired to hear the word, what worker can we compare with one who is anxious for the knowledge of eternal things?   Yet so that faith is not wanting to the work of the one, nor work to the knowledge of the other, as in the case of Mary ; lest either the leaves be without fruit, or the fruit without its natural protection be uncovered and open to injury."

Ambrose has no doubt about the Messianic import of the Psalms. We find him distinctly laying it down in the Preface to the Enarration on the 1st Psalm, § 8 :—

"What others announced by dark sayings appears to be plainly and openly promised to him [David] alone, that the Lord Jesus should be born of his seed, as the Lord said to him, *Of the fruit of thy body shall I set upon thy seat.* In the Psalms, therefore, not only is Jesus born for us, but also takes on Him the health-giving Passion, rests, rises again, ascends to heaven, sits at the right hand of the Father. What no man had taken upon himself to say, this Prophet alone announced, and afterwards the Lord Himself declared in the Gospel."

And he carries this principle out to the full :—

Ps. xxxvi. 9.—"Rightly it is said *In Thy light shall we see light,* according to the saying, *He that hath seen Me hath seen the Father.* With Thee, therefore, O Well of Life, we shall see the Father present. For as Thou wast with the Father in the beginning, God the Word, so the Father Who is in Thee is always with Thee, for He is with Him in Whom He is. And the Advent of our Lord and Saviour is foretold, Who at His coming on earth declared, *I and My Father are One,* that is, We are One Light, as We are One Name. We are Both One by unity of Light and Name ; or rather the Trinity is One by unity of substance, but with the difference of each Person. Trinity signifies a difference of Persons, Unity signifies Power. It might be said to the Father too, *For with Thee is the well of life,* that is, the Word was in Thee from Whom life proceeded, and always was, because He was with

Thee. *All things were made by Him* and in Him ; and He is the Life of all, and has manifested Thee to us, that men's hearts may be illuminated unto the knowledge of Thy Majesty."

Ps. xxxviii. 10.—" Lastly, that you may know it is rather to be understood of Christ, he has added, *As for the light of mine eyes it also is gone from me.* Who is the true light of all but Christ Jesus, of Whom John says, *That was the true Light which lighteth every man that cometh into the world ?* for He it is Who lightens both the bodily eyes and the mental vision. Let us beg therefore that He will always pour His light into us, and always be with us, as He was with David, who therefore ventured to say, *For with Thee is the well of life, and in Thy light shall we see light.* He, indeed, as a prophet had seen a great light : may his lantern shine for us, that we may not err. And the Word is a lantern, as the Word is the true Light, which lighteneth the whole world. *Lord, Thy Word is a lantern unto my feet.*"

Ps. xl. 10.—" *In the volume of the book it is written of Me.* Yes, it is written of Christ in the beginning of the Old Testament that He should come, to do the will of God the Father in the redemption of mankind ; since it is written that He formed Eve, in the likeness of the Church, to be a help to man. For what can be a defence to us, in the weakness of our body and the troubles of these times, but only the grace given to the Church, whereby we are redeemed, and our faith, by which we live? *In the volume of the book it is written : Bone of my bones and flesh of my flesh. Therefore shall a man leave his father and his mother, and shall cleave unto his wife ;*

and they shall be one flesh. Listen to one who tells us who is speaking, and to what the mystery refers; *This is a great mystery; but I speak concerning Christ and the Church.*"

Ps. xli. 9.—"What is *hath laid great wait for me?* The Greek has a word meaning *hath magnified;* and the Lord has movingly explained both words in the gospel, saying, *He that eateth bread with me hath lifted up his heel against me.* . . . When I was a boy I saw a wrestler after throwing his adversary strike his forehead with his heel, which was a remarkable thing, because in it he insulted the vanquished. And this is the meaning of the saying, *hath laid great wait for me;* by this word the Lord declares the arrogance of one who insulted Him. Judas lifted up his heel against Christ when he betrayed Him, but he did not lift it up unpunished. Adam still lifts up the heel which was wounded by the serpent. Christ, indeed, had washed the feet of Judas, and he had heard Him say, *He that is washed needeth not save to wash his feet, but is clean every whit.* But what grace washed, treachery had polluted. Judas, therefore, lifted up his heel to his wounding. He did not truly hold the Head who lifted up his heel against Christ. Adam lifted up his heel against himself, Judas his against Christ, and therefore the serpent wounded him more grievously than others. He lifted up his heel, who offered the treacherous kiss, to lay wait for his Master; and therefore it is written in the prophet, *hath laid great wait for me.* He who lays wait practises some trick by which he throws or wounds his adversary.

Therefore Judas is said to have laid wait, because by his kiss he inflicted a wound, by which he gave the persecutors a sign to rush upon the Saviour. So he laid wait like a serpent; because a serpent injects venom with his mouth, and wounds the heel with his fangs; and Judas wounded not the Divinity of Christ, but the end of the heel of His body. And Judas, too, lifted up his heel like a proud and insolent wrestler, in order to smite the Saviour's head; but he could not strike the head of Christ, for *the head of Christ is God.* He bound his own head with the knot of the hideous halter, to take away from himself the means of salvation."

The exposition on the 44th Psalm has a melancholy interest for us. It was the last work of the great Milanese prelate, the unswerving champion of the faith. It was never delivered; its concluding sentences were dictated and committed to writing only a few days before his decease. And in it he is still true to his principle; he still sees Jesus in the Psalter, with a spiritual sight not darkened by the weakness of the failing body, but intensified in its keenness by the nearer approach of the brightness of eternal day. Commenting on ver. 11 of this Psalm, *Thou hast given us like sheep appointed for meat,* he says: "Our good Lord Jesus Christ was made a sheep for our banqueting. Do you ask how? Listen to one who says, *Christ our Passover is sacrificed for us;* and consider how our forefathers in figure divided and ate the lamb, signifying the Passion of the Lord Jesus, on Whose sacrament we feed daily. Through the Sheep Himself, therefore, they became *flocks for meat*, as Aquila says ; or *flocks for eating*, as Theodotion expresses it ; or *pasture of the eaters*, as Symmachus has it. But a good banqueting is not to be feared, but to be desired by the saints ; for otherwise one cannot arrive at the kingdom of heaven, since the Lord Himself has said, *Except ye eat My flesh, and drink My blood, ye shall not have eternal life.* It is clear, therefore, that our Lord is the meat, the banquet, the nourishment of the eaters, as He Himself says, *I am the living Bread which came down from heaven.* And that you may know that, since He so came down, all has been done for our sake, the holy Apostle says, *We are all one bread.* Let us not fear, then, because we are become *sheep appointed for meat.* For as the flesh and blood of the Lord Himself has redeemed us, so also Peter, and the holy Apostle Paul too, and the other apostles, endured much for the Church when they were beaten with rods, stoned, and thrust into prison. For the Lord's people are made to stand firm, and the Church has gained her increase by their endurance of injuries and experience of dangers ; since others hastened to martyrdom, seeing that no loss befell the apostles by their sufferings, but that by (the sacrifice of) this short life they gained immortality."

So, again, on Ps. xlvi. 5. *God shall help her, and that right early*, he explains "right early" with a minuteness equal to that of the acknowledged interpretation of the xxii. Psalm.

" By this is signified that the resurrection early in the morning brings us heavenly aid, driving away the night and restoring the day, as the Scripture says, *Awake, thou that sleepest, and arise from the dead, and Christ shall give thee light.* See the mystery. Christ suffered towards eventide; therefore it was that according to the law the lamb was slain towards eventide. It was in the morning that He rose; for so it is written, *the first day of the week cometh Mary Magdalene early, when it was yet dark, unto the sepulchre, and seeth the stone taken away from the sepulchre.* Towards the evening of the world He is slain, when the light was beginning to fail; for the whole world was in darkness and would have been wrapped in more miserable darkness still, had not Christ, the Everlasting Light, come to us from heaven to pour out on mankind a season of innocence. So the Lord Jesus suffered, and pardoned our sins by His own blood; the light of a purer conscience shone out, and the day of spiritual grace beamed forth. Whence also the Apostle says, *The night is far spent, the day is at hand.*"

And on Ps. xlviii. 2 :—

"*Beautiful for situation, the joy of the whole earth, is mount Zion, on the sides of the north, the city of the Great King.* Why she is the joy of the whole earth is clearly expressed; it is because the Lord Jesus has gathered for Himself a Church from among sinners. Therefore those who before were *the sides of the north,* that is, associates and adherents of the devil, to whom it is said, *Awake, O north wind, and come, thou south,* are made the faithful in Christ. For of them is it said, *They that trust in the Lord shall be as Mount Zion ;* and so they become the Mount Zion

by the grace of Christ and the sacrament of baptism."

Christ is the key to a difficult passage, Psalm
xlix. 14 :—

"*Like sheep they are laid in the grave; death shall
feed on them; and the upright shall have dominion
over them in the morning; and their beauty shall con-
sume in the grave from their dwelling.* Those who
would not let Christ feed them, *death shall feed on
them.* Who then would drive away the Good Shepherd,
Who lays down His life for His sheep, because the
care of His flock pertains to Him? Or who would
choose death the hireling, to be brought to him with
the due reward of deeds of wickedness? Know, O
man, that Christ is the true Shepherd, Who feeds unto
life. Death has entered, and leads some to destruction, and devours those over whom it is able to prevail
because of their sins. Though they have in this life
eagerly pursued wealth and favour, that they might
have dominion over others, yet in the resurrection
servitude shall be theirs, when the brightness of the
morning dawns on the righteous, the figure of whom
is Jacob, set as a lord over his brother. And a
miserable servitude it will be, that, at the time when
others are called into the glory of light and splendour,
their glory will be waning and consuming in the
darkness of the grave."

On the Latin and Greek rendering of Psalm lxii. 1,
Shall not my soul be subject unto God? (*A.V., Truly
my soul waiteth upon God*), Ambrose 'takes occasion
to make an affectionate reference, at some length, to
the memory of the pious Gratian, murdered in 383,

some six years and more before the date of the
enarration (A.D. 390). And, as the versions agree in
reading for the words we translate *they delight in lies*
something which they rendered *I ran in thirst*, he
remarks on the guilty thirst of the tyrant who, as he
declares, devised at a banquet the murder of his
imperial prisoner. But he has first shown the
reference of the first verse to Christ, and guarded
against misapprehension :—

" Subjection then is the supereminence of human
virtue, not the diminution of Divine power. For if
they say that the Son is less than and not equal to
the Father, because He was subject to God the Father,
is He therefore less than His mother, because He
was subject to His mother ? for we read of Joseph
and Mary, *And He was subject unto them.* However,
we do not lose but gain by that affection of His through
which the Lord Jesus has infused grace and faith into
us all, that He may make us with faithful spirit subject
to God the Father. Therefore with a new and profound meaning the Apostle says that He will be
subject unto the Father in us, when there is in all the
fulness of faith, and a kind of unity in devotion.
For now, so long as we differ in opinion, we in a
manner lessen Christ's kingdom ; for all things are
not yet subject to Him whose kingdom is unity : but
*when all things shall be subdued unto Him, then shall
the Son also Himself be subject unto Him That put all
things under Him, that God may be all in all,* as it is
written. For now He is above all in power ; but it is
needful that He be in all by will, and this will He will
have when He knows all that is within us to be full of

Him and void of sin. Christ is not therefore yet subject to the Father, because He is not yet all in all ; but when Christ is all in all, God will be all in all. Whence we gather that the kingdom of the Father, and of the Son, and of the Holy Ghost is one : because He who receives the Son receives also the Father and the Holy Ghost : for the power, grace, and operation of the Trinity is one."

It is perhaps in the Exposition on the 119th Psalm that the powers of the preacher and commentator are best seen. The work belongs to A.D. 385-6 ; years of bitter persecution for the bishop at the hand of Justina and the Arian party. Besides explaining the Psalm, which he considered as a sort of miniature of the whole Psalter, he quotes freely from the rest of the Psalms, and from other books both of the Old and New Testament, expounding as he quotes. He uses the Canticles so largely that the chief part of the comment on that book which has been compiled from his works is drawn from this portion of them. The literal, moral, and mystical senses have each of them their due amount of attention ; and the heretic, the Jew, and the philosopher alike become in turn the object of the preacher's burning words. Sometimes, it is true, the illustrations are quaint, but they are always telling :—

(Verses 153—160). "Here begins the 20th letter Res (Resh), which is interpreted by the Latin word signifying 'head' or 'primacy.' . . . All the vigour of life and grace of beauty is in the head. The snake is said, when it is pressed by danger, always to hide its head, and, coiling itself into a circle, to

defend this part alone, leaving the rest of the body
exposed ; because it is said that if the vigour of the
head be preserved, it can repair the other members
when wounded. So do thou also keep the head, in
a moral sense, and in a mystical sense too. Christ is
the mystical Head, because *by Him all things consist,
and He is the Head of the body, the Church.* He who
has lost this Head will not be able to derive any
advantage from living. In this alone we, who are
formed after the image of God, and the likeness of
virtues, differ from brutes. Faith separates us from
being like to animals void of reason. O ye human
serpents, keep well this Head : though all the limbs
be beaten, the whole body burnt in the fire, plunged
in the deep, or torn by beasts, yet if this Head be
guarded, life is unhurt, and safety assured ; for no
one can perish from whom Christ is not taken away."

All hearts will thrill in unison with the sweet earnest
prayer he draws from the conclusion of the Psalm.

"*O seek Thy servants, for I do not forget Thy
commandments.* Come then, Lord Jesus, seek Thy
servant, seek Thy weary sheep ; come, O Shepherd,
seek *Joseph like a sheep.* Thy sheep has strayed whilst
Thou wert delaying and staying on the mountains.
Leave Thy ninety and nine, and come and seek the
one that has strayed. Come without dogs, come
without evil workers, come without the hireling who
knows not how to enter by the door. Come without
helper, without any to announce Thee ; I have long
waited for Thy coming. I know Thou wilt come,
for I do not forget Thy commandments. Come not
with a rod, but *in love and in the spirit of meekness.*"

L

The ten books of "Expositions" on the gospel of
St. Luke are rightly called by this name rather than
by that of Commentary. They are by no means a
complete comment, but rather a series of sermonets
on certain passages of St. Luke, arranged in the order
of the gospel itself, or, as we should say, according to
chapter and verse. Their date of publication is fixed
at the same year of troubles and persecutions (386)
as the Enarrations on the 119th Psalm; they were
probably delivered orally during the two years immediately preceding their collection into a whole.
Auxentius the Arian is not indistinctly alluded to in
the comments on x. 3 : *I send you forth as lambs
among wolves.* And on *"wars and commotions"*
(xxi. 9) we have another historical illustration :—

"None are better witnesses to the heavenly words
than ourselves, on whom the end of the world is
come. What wars and what rumours of wars we
have known ! The Huns rose against the Alans, the
Alans against the Goths, the Goths against the Tay-
fali and Sarmatæ. The exiles of the Goths have
made us too in Illyricum exiles from our fatherland,
and *the end is not by-and-by.* How universal has been
famine, and epidemic, among oxen and other cattle,
as well as among men ! so that even in the case of
those of us who have not endured war, pestilence has
made us like people crushed by war."

There is a difference of opinion about the merits of
the Expositions. According to Rufinus, St. Jerome
(one of the most captious of critics) alluded to this
commentary when he said that of two works of
Ambrose one was dull both in sense and language,

the other sportive in words but sleepy in meaning.
But Jerome was particularly and unreasonably jealous
of Ambrose. It is true, however, that the expositions
on St. Luke, though valuable, and full of thought and
sound theology, are not so lively and sparkling as
those on the Psalms. The author revelled in the
mystical, and seems therefore under constraint when
he is, by the nature of his text, rather confined to the
literal or moral. In fact, he takes every opportunity
of breaking away from his restraint into something at
least allegorical or figurative, if not absolutely mystical.
In dealing with the 3rd verse of the 1st chapter, he
cannot speak of the deposit of the Gospel committed
to Theophilus, "one whom God loves," without a
figurative interpretation of the moth and rust which
we are bound carefully to prevent from corrupting it.
The rust is covetousness, carelessness, worldly ambition : Photinus, Arius, Sabellius, the spirit of antichrist which denies the Incarnation, are moths that
lacerate the sacred vestures in the store. Again, the
food of the Baptist is significant. Ambrose does not,
as a modern preacher or lecturer might do, give a
graphic sketch of life in the wilderness, investigate
the nature of the locusts and the wild honey, and
discuss the question between the vegetarian and the
opposite view, but works out a somewhat far-fetched
meaning:—

"The food of the prophet is a mark of his office,
and tells of a mystery. What so useless, in respect
of a man's duty, as catching locusts, and what so full
of meaning in respect of prophetic mystery? For
locusts, the more unprofitable, idle, fleeting, wandering,

noisy they are, the more fitly they represent the
Gentiles, who, without labour or profitable work,
without dignity, without voice, utter a melancholy
sound, but know nothing of the word of life. This
people is the food of prophets, because the larger the
number of them congregated together, the more plentiful the advantage of prophetic speech. And the
grace of the Church is prefigured in the wild honey,
not found by the Jewish people in the hive of the
law, but scattered, by the wandering of the Gentiles,
over the fields, and the leaves of the forest, as it is
written, *We found it in the fields of the wood.*"

Of a similar character,—not historical, but figurative,—is his explanation of the difficult word in vi. 1,
rendered in our version "second Sabbath after the
first," but literally "second-first Sabbath."

"It is curious that St. Luke says 'second-first,' not
'first-second,' for that which is best ought to be put
first. It is the second, because a first according to
the law went before it, and there was a punishment
prescribed if any one worked on it; it is the first,
because the Sabbath according to the law, which was
first, is done away, and this, which was ordained
second, has become the first. For as it is lawful to
work on the Sabbath, and there is no punishment for
one who works, the very name of Sabbath did not
remain, its force according to the law being done
away. However, though one was first in order, the
other in principle, the latter was not therefore less
than the former, for the first Adam is not to be compared with the second Adam; *the first man Adam
was made a living soul; the last Adam was made*

a quickening spirit . . . the first man is of the earth earthy; the second Man is the Lord from heaven. The second was preferred before the first, for one was the cause of death, the other of life. So also we have the word 'second-first' Sabbath; second in number, first in grace; for the Sabbath in which men are exempted from punishment is better than that for which a punishment is prescribed. The law is first, the Gospel second; but fear is lower than grace."

Even a remark of St. Paul which we should look upon as to be understood literally, and literally only, is made to bear a figurative sense :—

"*It may be,* he says, *that I will abide, yea, and winter with you;* and farther on, *But I will tarry at Ephesus until Pentecost, for a great door is opened unto me.* He winters with the Corinthians, because he was troubled with their errors, and their affection toward the service of God was cold; he keeps Pentecost with the Ephesians, and imparts to them mysteries, and refreshes his soul, because he sees them to be glowing with the warmth of faith."

A similar exposition is made, incidentally, of the remark in St. John xviii. 18 :—

"*It was cold.* If we consider the time of year, it could not be cold, but the cold was where Jesus was not confessed, where there was none to see the light, where He was denied Who *is a consuming fire.* So the cold was that of the mind, not of the body. Lastly, Peter stood near the coals because he was cold in heart. The Jewish flame is hurtful, it burns, but does not give warmth. The fire is hurtful which sprinkles the soot of error (so to speak) even over the minds of saints, at which even Peter's inward eyes were darkened. Those were not eyes of flesh and blood, but eyes of the mind, with which he saw Christ."

The parable of the barren fig-tree, again, is explained mystically, not morally; the exposition, however, is not far-fetched, but most instructive and edifying :—

"*These three years I come seeking fruit on this fig-tree.* He came to Abraham, to Moses, to Mary; that is, He came in the sign, in the law, in the body. We recognise His coming by its benefits. In one there is purification, in another sanctification, in another justification; circumcision purified, the law sanctified, grace justified. One was in all, and all in One. For none can be cleansed, but he who fears the Lord; none is fit to receive the law but he who is purified from fault; none comes near to grace but he who knows the law. Therefore the Jewish people could neither be purified, because they had the circumcision of the body, not of the heart; nor be sanctified, because they knew not the virtue of the law, following the carnal rather than the spiritual (*for we know that the law is spiritual*); nor be justified, because they did not repent of their offences, and therefore knew nothing of grace. Justly, therefore, no fruit was found in the synagogue, and therefore it is commanded to be cut down."

It is curious to light on a little confusion of names which we are hardly prepared for in so accurate a theologian, though it does not justify the sweeping condemnation of the critic. Just as Polycrates and Clement of Alexandria confounded Philip the deacon

with Philip the apostle, and claimed the latter with
St. Peter as an apostolic precedent for marriage, so
Ambrose fails to distinguish the two (or three) who
bear the name of James. There went up into the
mount of transfiguration, he says, "Peter, who received the keys of the kingdom of heaven; John,
to whom is committed the Lord's mother; James,
who first ascended the episcopal throne." Whether
James, the Lord's brother, first bishop of Jerusalem,
James the less, James the son of Alphæus, are one
or two persons, is not by any means a settled point;
but Ambrose is clearly wrong in speaking of the son
of Zebedee as first bishop.

Another mistake, or misconception, on the part of
the commentator is justly criticised by Jerome. He
joins with St Hilary of Poictiers (on St. Matthew
xxvi. 70) in a strange piece of special pleading in
favour of St. Peter in his denial of our Lord; and all
will probably agree with Jerome's caustic remark that
it defends the erring disciple at the expense of the
truthfulness of Him who said *Thou shalt deny Me
thrice.*

" But let us consider the form of his denial, which
I see to be differently stated by the different evangelists. It was so new a thing for Peter to be able to
sin, that his sin could not be understood by the evangelists. Therefore, when the maid stated to Peter
that he was of those who were with Jesus of Nazareth,
Matthew has set down that he first replied, *I know not
what thou sayest.* So also Mark, who followed Peter,
and may have learnt more accurately of him. This
is the first utterance of Peter in his denial; but he

does not seem in it to deny the Lord, but to withdraw himself from the woman's betrayal of him. And consider what he denied; it was his being of those who were with Jesus of Galilee, or as Mark puts it, with Jesus of Nazareth. Did he deny having been with the Son of God? It was only saying, I know Him not as Galilean or Nazarene whom I know as the Son of God. . . . Being asked, *Art thou also one of those who were with Jesus of Galilee?* he shrank from the word of eternity; for those who had a beginning of being 'were' not, that is to say, He alone was Who was in the beginning. Finally, he says, *I am not;* for it belongs to Him alone to be Who is always. Whence also Moses says, *I AM hath sent me.* . . . Lastly, according to Matthew, being pointed out as having been with Jesus, he said, *I know not the man.* . . . And he rightly denied Him as man whom he knew to be God. . . . John has set it down thus, that being asked by the maid whether he were one of that man's disciples, he first replied *I am not.* He who was Christ's was not a man's apostle. In fact, Paul also declared himself to be no man's apostle, saying, *Paul, an apostle, not of men, neither by man, but by Jesus Christ and God the Father.* . . . The answer is consistent in every case; for he who said *I know not the man,* replied properly enough when asked whether he were of 'the man's' disciples, *I am not.* He did not therefore deny himself to be Christ's disciple, but a man's disciple. So both Peter and Paul denied Him as man Whom they confessed to be the Son of God. . . . Luke also has written that Peter, when asked whether he was of them, answered at first, *I know Him not.* And he spoke well; for it were rash to say he knew Him whom the mind of man cannot comprehend; for *no man knoweth the Son but the Father.* Again, in his second reply, according to Luke, Peter said, *I am not.* He had rather, you see, deny himself than Christ.... . And at the third question he said, *I know not what thou sayest,* that is, ' I know nothing of your sacrilege.' "

The expositor himself is hardly satisfied with his defence of the apostle, for he goes on thus :—

" We excuse him, but he made no excuse ; for an ambiguous answer does not beseem one who confesses Jesus, but an open confession. What use is there in employing ambiguous words, if you wish to appear to have made a denial? So Peter is represented as not having answered thus of set purpose, because *when he thought thereon he wept.*"

His defence of Peter is, however, not owing to anything approaching to the modern Roman view of papal supremacy. He treated Damasus, as we know, with respectful courtesy, but by no means submissively; and in the same spirit he deals with the passage (St. Matt. xvi. 18) which was naturally present to his mind when explaining the corresponding portion of St. Luke (ix. 20) :—

" The Rock is Christ ; *for they drank of that spiritual Rock that followed them, and that Rock was Christ;* and He did not refuse to His disciple the grace of that word, so that he too should be Peter, as having from the Rock (petra) solidity of endurance, firmness of faith. Strive therefore that thou also mayst be a rock. Therefore look for the rock, not out of thyself, but in thyself. . . . Thy rock is faith, the foundation of the Church is faith. If thou be a rock, thou wilt be in the Church, for the Church is on a rock. If thou be in the Church, the gates of hell will not prevail against thee. The gates of hell are the gates of death, and the gates of death cannot be the gates of the Church."

Of the more literal part of the expositions, which, as has been already observed, though valuable, is not so brilliant as the comment on the Psalms, space will allow but two specimens. One is the explanation of the discrepancy between the later part of the two genealogies of the evangelists Matthew and Luke.

"We remark that St. Matthew has stated that Jacob, father of Joseph, was son of Matthan; Luke that Joseph, the husband of Mary, was son of Heli, and he has described Heli as being son of Melchi. How can there be two fathers, Heli and Jacob, to one man? and how two paternal grandfathers, Matthan and Melchi? But if you search accurately, you will find that according to the rule of the old law two brothers were fathers of two half-brothers by one wife. For it is related that Matthan, who was descended from Solomon, had a son Jacob, and died, leaving a wife living. Melchi then married her, and she had a son Heli; again Heli, his brother dying without issue, took his brother's wife, and had a son Joseph, who according to the law is called son of Jacob."

The other passage is one containing his views on one point at least of what we now term eschatology. He seems, like Gregory of Nyssa and John of

Damascus, to be following the teaching of Origen, his favourite.

"He who does not bring peace and love to Christ's altar shall be bound hand and foot, and taken and *cast into outer darkness; there shall be weeping and gnashing of teeth.* What is the outer darkness? Are there any prisons or quarries to be undergone there? By no means. But all who are outside the promises of the heavenly commands are in outer darkness, because the commandments of God are light, and whoever is without Christ is in darkness, because Christ is *light in the darkness.* Therefore there is no gnashing of bodily teeth, nor any perpetual fire with bodily flame, nor any bodily worm. But these phrases are used, because as fever and worms are produced from indigestion, so if any one does not digest his sins, by the interposition of sobriety and abstinence, but by mingling sin with sin brings on a sort of indigestion with offences old and new, he will be burnt with fire of his own, and consumed by his own worms. Whence also Isaiah says, *Walk in the light of your fire, and in the sparks that ye have kindled.* The fire is that produced by sorrow for crime; the worm is this, that the sins of the irrational soul afflict the mind and sense of the guilty, and, as it were, prey on the bowels of his conscience; and these are engendered like worms in each man, as if from the body of the sinner. In fact, the Lord has declared the same by Isaiah, saying, *They shall look upon the carcases of the men that have transgressed against Me; for their worm shall not die, neither shall their fire be quenched.*"

THE HEXAEMERON (A.D. 389).—The idea, and much of the material, of these six sets of discourses on the history of the Six Days of Creation, as given in Gen. i., are taken from the Hexaëmeron of St. Basil. But Ambrose does not slavishly adhere to his model; Origen and Hippolytus were evidently in his mind as he wrote, and he not only refers to Aristotle and Plato, but quotes Virgil and Pliny by name. Indeed, it is palpable that he had the Georgics by heart.

The object of Moses, or rather of Him Who inspired Moses, was, he says, not to give us scientific truths, nor to introduce us to the wisdom of the Egyptians, but to teach us about God and our hope in Jesus Christ. Yet the preacher cannot help diverging into science and natural history, though he generally endeavours to defend the divergence by some moral lesson or mystical exposition drawn from physical truth. *In the beginning*, he tells us, means "in Christ," for *all things were made by Him, and without Him was not anything made.* The sun represents Christ, and the moon the Church: *the sun knoweth his going down,* refers to the Passion; *He appointed the moon for certain seasons,* to the vicissitudes of the Church, her alternating seasons of persecution and peace. The *gathering together of waters* tells of the Church, gathered from the valleys of heresy and heathenism, and the morasses of self-indulgence and impurity, into a community which is *founded upon the seas and prepared upon the floods,* so that *the floods have lifted up their voice, the floods lift up their waves* to the Lord of all. Beasts, birds, fishes, reptiles, insects, all have their moral or mystical lessons to teach us; and the vine, and the fig-tree, and the very grass of the field are not without their warnings and their promises.

One reads with interest, not unmixed with amusement, the scientific belief of an educated Roman and Greek gentleman of the fourth century as contained in these remarkable discourses. Ambrose is no Darwinian: matter, he says, is not uncreated, but had a commencement *in the beginning*, that is, before time began. It was created in the rough, and in disorder, and moulded into regular form, that God might display His power to arrange as well as to create. Each plant and animal is produced *after his kind* by a perpetual ordinance of the Author of all; and peculiarities, such as the neck of the camel and the trunk and legs of the elephant, are the special creation of God. Ambrose holds that the world is spherical; that the sun is naturally and not accidentally hot, and that light must be distinguished from the sun, being prior to the sun; that the moon influences the tides; that eclipses of the moon are caused by the earth's shadow; that the circumference of the earth is about 180,000 stadia (22,000 miles). He considers the brain to be the centre of the nervous system, and the heart of the arterial, and has in other respects a fairly correct idea of human physiology. He is acquainted with the mode of respiration in insects and fishes, knows the habits of the hippopotamus and the elephant, and is aware of the value of opium as a medicine. He argues most sensibly against astrology and the fatalism which it

necessarily implies: once admit its principle, he
says, "and you cannot praise a good man or con-
demn a bad one, since each appears to correspond
to the necessity of his nativity"; Jonah was cast into
the sea, and afterwards rescued, the penitent thief
saved, the Apostles converted, St. Peter delivered
from prison, St. Paul cured of his blindness, and preserved from the viper, not by the power of a natal
star, but by the providence and grace of God. With
all these correct and reasonable notions we have, on
the other hand, the most extraordinary fancies, mis-
apprehensions, and fallacies. He holds, of course,
the doctrine of the four elements, though he rejects
the idea of the fifth, or quintessence. He believes,
or tells as if he believed, the old tales of the phœnix
and the halcyon; of the lion being terrified at a
white cock, and being cured of sickness by eating a
monkey; of the elephant dreading a mouse, of the
bear licking its cubs into shape, of the wolf striking
a man dumb by looking at him unseen, of the eagle
holding up its young to see if they can face the sun
unmoved, with this addition, that the rejected eaglets
are taken and brought up by the coot. Quails, he
says, feed on hellebore; blackberry leaves thrown on
a serpent will kill it; vultures do not pair; snakes
cure blindness with fennel; tortoises eat serpents,
and, if poisoned, take marjoram as an antidote; the
cicada sings loudest at mid-day, because at that time
the air is purer. He gives a receipt worth trying,
though it is to be feared he attributes too much virtue
to it; mosquitoes, he tells us, can be kept off by
the use of an ointment made of wormwood boiled in

oil. The Suez Canal, one of the great facts of our own days, is considered by him as an impossibility, after the failures of Sesostris and Darius; but no doubt a railroad and an electric telegraph would have been placed in the same category.

The work is a strange tissue of facts and fancies, of the literal and the mystical, of science and religion. And yet there is in it nothing ridiculous, and much that is admirable. The power and wisdom of God and the truth of Scripture are upheld in almost every page; and, like a true evangelical teacher, Ambrose finds Christ everywhere. We have seen how Christ was for him "the beginning": he not only begins, but ends with the Saviour; for his conclusion runs thus :—

"Thanks, then, to our Lord God, who has made a work in which to rest. He made the heaven, I do not read that He rested; He made the earth, I do not read that He rested; He made the sun, moon, and stars, I do not read even then that He rested: but I read that He made man, and then He rested, having one whose sins He might forgive. Or, perhaps, there was then a mystical intimation of our Lord's coming Passion, in which it was revealed that Christ was resting in man, appointing for Himself a rest in the body, for the redemption of man, as He Himself said, *I laid Me down and slept, and rose up again, for the Lord sustained Me.*"

ON PARADISE (A.D. 375).—This book, or rather set of sermons, is believed to be the earliest of Ambrose's works. The discourses were delivered

and collected in the year immediately following
his consecration.   There is observable in them a
kind of juvenility of style, which is much what we
should expect to find in the first sermons of a
neophyte bishop of five-and-thirty.   He is evidently
indebted to Philo, whom, indeed, he mentions by
name, remarking that as a Jew he could not comprehend the spiritual sense of the Scriptures, but was
compelled to confine himself to their bearing on
morals.   While not rejecting the literal sense of the
Scripture on which he is commenting, Ambrose permits, and inclines to, an interpretation partly mystical,
partly allegorical.   The garden of Eden is the holy
soul ; the river that waters it is Christ.   Pison, Gihon,
Hiddekel, and Phrath (the Ganges, the Nile, the
Tigris, and the Euphrates) represent the four virtues
of wisdom, purity, courage, and righteousness, which
characterize the four ages of the world ; the period
from the Creation to the Deluge being that of wisdom, that from the Deluge to the Law the age of
purity, the time of the Law the period of courage,
and that of the Gospel the age of righteousness.   The
serpent is pleasure, Eve sense, Adam intellect ; and
the temptation represents to us the depravation of
the intellectual man through the allurements of sensual gratification.   This interpretation the writer
adheres to in a letter to his friend Sabinus, some
years later.   He next proceeds to examine a number
of heretical and infidel questions asked and objec-
tions raised.   The most important is an objection or
difficulty which takes this form : " Did God know or
not that Adam would disobey ? if not, His wisdom is

not infinite; if He did, He gave a superfluous and useless command." The answer is, God, though He foreknew Adam's transgression, did not lay on him any necessity of transgressing, any more than He laid on Judas a necessity of betraying his Master. Both might have abstained from sin : the fault lies with the transgressor, not the giver of the commandment. God is not unrighteous, who permits humanity to be tried. How then, it is asked, since the woman was the cause of man's fall, do we find it said of Adam in his solitude, *It is not good*, while man created male and female is pronounced *very good*? The reply is that the woman was to be God's instrument in producing souls whom He might save, and still more in producing the Saviour of those souls; for it is written, *she shall be saved in child-bearing*, a promise which undoubtedly relates to the Messiah.

The allegorical exposition is here taken up again. God walking in the garden is to be understood of His varied modes of presence through the Holy Scriptures, and of His varied dealings with the soul. The question put to Adam, *Where art thou?* inquired not about his place, but his spiritual condition; "How low has thy sin brought thee, that thou fliest from thy God!" And, lastly, the curse on the serpent, *on thy belly shalt thou go*, signifies the degraded character of sensuality, and *dust shalt thou eat*, the fact that it has to do with the earthly and bodily, not with the spirit.

The book ends abruptly. It is extremely probable that the last discourses on the Fall have not come down to us. We look in vain for an explanation of the coats of skins, the guard set over the tree of life, and, above all, of the Messianic promise, *It shall bruise thy head, and thou shalt bruise His heel.*

CAIN AND ABEL.—This treatise, or set of discourses, belongs also to the year 375, and is, we are told at the outset, a continuation of the book on Paradise. We observe in it the same juvenility of style, and the same, or even greater, indebtedness to Philo. The interpretation is allegorical throughout. Ambrose begins by showing that Cain and Abel represent respectively the worldly-minded and the religious, and are a figure of the Synagogue and the Church. He then digresses, and rambles freely, remarking discursively on Abraham, Isaac, Esau, Jacob, Moses (whom he believes to have been translated, not really dead and buried), and Pharaoh. Returning to the point, he gives us a somewhat more literal comment. The offerings of Cain and Abel furnish an opportunity of giving advice on the subject of prayer: we should offer to God the best produce of our souls, and offer carefully: "Take care not to speak without thought, for the lips of the thoughtless lead him into evil; take care not to extol thyself in prayer, for the prayer of him that humbleth himself shall pierce the clouds; take care not to divulge unwarily the mysteries of the Creed or Lord's Prayer; knowest thou not how grievous it is to commit sin in prayer, where thou hopest for a remedy? Surely the Lord has taught by the prophet that this is a grievous curse, saying, *Let his prayer be turned into sin.*" The Hebrew words which we render, *If thou doest well, shalt thou not be accepted? and if thou doest not well, sin lieth at the door*, are turned in the LXX. and Latin into, *If thou offer aright, but divide not aright, thou hast sinned; be still:* and the passage is explained thus: Cain offered aright, but he did not divide aright, for he offered not readily and quickly, but *in process of time;* and of the fruit only, not, like Abel, of the first-fruits. After the murder, we are told to remark, it is not the loving brother, but *the voice of thy brother's blood* that calls for vengeance: and the fratricide dreads temporal death more than eternal judgment, while God spares him in mercy, to give him space for repentance.

NOAH AND THE ARK.—This work appears to have been completed in 379, during the troublous time following on the defeat and death of Valens, when the author had himself just recovered from a dangerous illness, and was lamenting the decease of his only brother. Like the foregoing books, it contains evident traces of Philo. It has come to us in an imperfect state: the conclusion is as abrupt as that of the Paradise; there are at least two palpable lacunæ; and St. Augustine twice quotes a passage from it which is not found in our text.

Ambrose in this book distinguishes expressly between the literal and the "higher" sense; and in his remarks on the various portions of the narrative is careful to give each, first explaining the literal meaning with its practical teaching, then stating the allegorical significance. Of the spiritual sense, strangely enough, we find nothing: of Noah as a type of Christ, and the Ark as prefiguring the Church, there is not a single word.

For the "gopher" or cypress wood, the material of the ark, the LXX. has "squared" planks; the Vulgate renders it "smoothed" planks. St. Ambrose's Latin version follows the Greek; and he takes occasion from the word to institute an extraordinary comparison between the fabric of the ark and that of the human body. According to the "higher" sense, which he then proceeds to develop, the opening of the windows of heaven signifies mental trouble, the breaking up of the fountains of the great deep the perturbation of the body and its senses. The waters prevail *fifteen cubits upward*, to show how all the senses of men are overpowered by the flood of passion; for (he explains) there are five senses, and each of them is threefold, comprising object, subject, and act (as, for example, sight sees the visible); the senses, therefore, are properly represented by thrice five. The clean beasts mean the senses of the wise man, the clean fowls his thoughts; the raven is vice, which loves the blood of passion and finds a home in it; the dove is virtue, which cannot rest in the flood, but returns to the soul with the olive-leaf of peace, and does not consent to dwell on the earth till the tide of evil has passed away. *As the green herb have I given you all things* proves, according to the letter, the lawfulness of eating some kinds of flesh: the higher sense is that irrational passions are to be as subject to the wise man as herbs to the gardener: the promise that there should no more be *a flood to destroy all flesh* implies that God will restrain the force of human passion; the bow in the cloud is His power, which like a bow is now drawn in

judgment, now slackened in mercy. Noah's drunkenness and nudity are not, as in the literal sense, an
offence and a warning, but a ground of praise ; for
they betoken the withdrawal of the wise from all
earthly thoughts and earthly gratifications.[1]   The
only Christian piece of symbolism occurs near the
end of the book, where the 350 years of Noah's life
after the Flood are treated of.   The 300, like the
same number in the 318 servants of Abraham (such
is the explanation given in the epistle attributed to
St. Barnabas and adopted by Ambrose in the book
on Abraham), is expressed by the Greek *tau*, the sign
of the cross, and so signifies Christ; the 50, the
jubilee number, represents the gift of the Spirit ; the
350 years therefore tell us of pardon and grace.

The two books on ABRAHAM, with several others,
belong to the year 387, the date of the baptism of
Augustine.   The idea of the work may possibly have
been taken from Philo, but not the language and
expressions.   In the first book Ambrose proposes to
follow the examples of Plato in his " Republic," and
Xenophon in his " Cyropædia."   They drew the
pattern of a perfect commonwealth and a perfect
man ; he will sketch a wise and religious character.
But their patterns were mere fiction ; his will be far
superior, being the true history of a real servant of
God.   So he goes through the Scriptural account of
Abraham's life, showing the practical lessons to be
learnt from it.   The typical is not forgotten : Sarah
is the Church, as St. Paul shows ; Isaac carrying the

---

[1] In the *Elijah* Ambrose accepts the literal sense (*see* p. 193).

wood is Christ bearing His cross; the ass on which
Isaac rode signifies the Gentiles; and in seeing all
this Abraham saw Christ; wherefore the Lord said,
*Abraham rejoiced to see My day; and he saw it, and
was glad.* We are warned, in reading that *God did
tempt Abraham,* not to confound God's temptations
with the devil's; "the devil tempts that he may ruin,
God that He may crown." And we find here and
there pieces of Christian counsel: bishops should be
hospitable, like Abraham; Christians ought not to
marry Jews or heathen; ladies are not to make the
earrings and bracelets of Rebekah a plea for excess
in jewellery.

The text of the second book is not perfect. In it
Ambrose designs not to give the practical, but the
allegorical meaning, or "higher sense," of the life of
Abraham, just as he did (he says) when writing of
Adam and Eve.

Abraham is the wise soul. It must quit the
"Haran" of earthly passion, and go to "Bethel,"
God's house, and there call upon His name; it may
be driven by stress of circumstances to "Egypt,"
temptation and trial, but will soon depart thence
"very rich," retaining all its virtues, and return to
Bethel; it will not be able to dwell with "Lot," a man
half inclined to sin, but will resign to him the earthly
joys of the "Jordan valley," and receive from God
the assurance of "possessing the whole land," since
nothing is wanting to the truly wise. When the
"four kings," the sensual pleasures derived from the
four elements, overpower the "five kings," or five
senses, and take the waverer Lot captive, the wise

soul, in the power of the " 318," that is, of the cross
of Jesus, will rescue him; and " Melchizedek," the
king of righteousness, will bestow His blessing. The
wise soul will take nothing of the earthly spoil, but
will, according to God's direction, offer to Him,
earth, sea, and air, or body, sense, and speech, under
the figure of the divided heifer, goat, and ram, together with the undivided dove and pigeon, signifying
purity and grace; the "smoking furnace," or be-
clouded humanity, which contemplates the offering,
will be followed by the "burning lamp" of heavenly
illumination; and God will promise to the progeny
of "Sarah," the Church, the possession of future
glory; the mark of her children on earth will be the
" circumcision," or entire purification of the Spirit.

To the same year belong ISAAC AND THE SOUL, and
THE BENEFIT OF DEATH. In the former Ambrose
passes on from the wedlock of Isaac and Rebekah to
the spiritual union between the soul and its Lord, the
Church and her Master, the Spouse and the Bride;
and at once enters upon a series of expositions on
texts from the Song of Songs, for which he is much
indebted to Origen's commentary on that book. One
of the most beautiful of the many sweet passages in
the comment is that on chap. v. ver. 2, 3 :—

"*I sleep, but my heart waketh.* . . . Though thou
be asleep, yet if Christ knows the devotion of thy
soul, He comes, and knocks at its door, and says,
Open to Me, My sister. Well is it said, *sister*, because
the marriage of the Word and the soul is spiritual.
Souls know nothing of wedlock and earthly bonds,
but are *as the angels in heaven.* *Open,* He says, *to*

Me, but shut against strangers; shut against the world. Come not forth to things material, leave not thine own light to seek another's; material light produces thick darkness, so that the brightness of true glory is not seen. *Open*, then, *to Me*, but open not to the enemy; do not give place to the devil. Open thyself to Me, be not straitened; open thyself wide, and I will fill thee. And since in going through the world I have found too much trouble and offence, and could not easily obtain a place to rest in, do thou open thyself, that the Son of Man may lay His head in thee, for He cannot rest save on the humble and meek. The soul hearing the cry, *Open to Me, My sister, My love, My dove, My undefiled, for My head is filled with dew*, that is, with worldly temptations, being suddenly disturbed, and ready to rise as she is bidden, replies, wafting the perfume of aloes and myrrh, the signs of burial, *I have put off my coat, how shall I put it on ? I have washed my feet, how shall I defile them?* She is afraid to rise up again to temptation, lest she come again to crime and sin, and begin to pollute her steps and the progress of her virtues with the traces of earth. Thus does she give proof of the perfection of her virtue, having won such love from Christ, that He comes to her, and knocks at her door, and comes with the Father, and sups with that soul, and she with Him, as John says in the Revelation. For having heard the call, *Come with Me from Lebanon, My spouse, with Me from Lebanon*, and knowing that in the flesh she cannot be with Christ, but is with Him if she is so in spirit, she conforms herself to His will, so as to be conformed to the image of Christ, and is no more conscious of the weeds of the flesh. . . . *I have put off my coat, how shall I put it on ?* She has put off that coat of skins which Adam and Eve received after their sin, that coat of corruption and passion. *How shall I put it on ?* She does not seek to put it on, but signifies that it is so cast away that it can be her clothing no more. *I have washed my feet, how shall I defile them ?* that is, I washed my feet when I came forth, and raised myself above that which is earthly : how shall I defile them by returning into the dark prison of passion ?"

In THE BENEFIT OF DEATH, Ambrose replies to the question, " As life is a good, must not its contrary, death, be an evil ? " Of death, he says, there are three kinds : 1. Death in sin, which is evil ; 2. Death to sin, which is good : 3. The Separation of body and soul, which is dreaded by some because it is called destruction, and because of the pagan horrors connected with the next world ; but it is really good, as being a deliverance from sorrow and danger, an end to sin, and the way to a better life. We must wait for it patiently, and practise it, so long as we are here, by self-denial and what is appropriately called mortification. He then quotes the second book of Esdras (vii. 32, 33) which he appears to consider as authentic and canonical, inquiring which was the earliest, Plato or Esdras, and asserting that St. Paul followed Esdras, and not Plato : and indeed, in a letter written in this year to his friend Horontianus, he recommends the study of the book. From the passage quoted he proceeds to lay down that departed souls remain, some in pain, some in bliss, till the Last Day. Of the bliss of the latter there are seven gradations, for it is written *every one in his own order*. The first is freedom from temptation, through victory over the flesh ; the second, freedom from care and dread ; the third, the being, through remembrance of obedience, without any fear of the judgment ; the fourth, rest in prevision of coming glory ; the fifth, the sense of light and freedom ; the sixth, the shining forth as the sun ; the seventh, the confident anticipation of the vision of God. Then comes the consummation of all, when " we shall go to those who are sitting down with Abraham, Isaac, and Jacob in the kingdom of God, because when bidden to the supper they did not make excuse. We shall go where is the paradise of joy, the garden of Eden, where the Adam who fell among thieves no longer weeps over his wounds, where the thief himself rejoices in his share of the heavenly kingdom, where there are no clouds, no thunder, no lightnings, no stormy wind, no darkness, no eventide, where neither summer nor winter will vary the seasons. There will be no frost, no hail, no rain, no need of yonder sun, or moon, or stars, but the brightness of God alone shall shine. For God will be the light of all ; and that *true Light which lighteth every man* shall beam on all. We shall go where the Lord Jesus has prepared mansions for His servants, that where He is we may be also. For so hath He willed it. Hear Him telling what those mansions are : *In My Father's house are many mansions ;* and what His will is : *I will come again*, saith He, *and receive you unto Myself, that where I am there ye may be also.*"

RETREAT FROM THE WORLD, OR, JACOB IN PADAN-ARAM, belongs also to the year 387, and, like many other works of Ambrose, owes not a little to Philo. Its object is, as the title shows, to point out the advantage of retirement from the pursuit of worldly things, and the withdrawal of the soul from the earth, as a sort of representation or practice of death while the body still remains in the world. Ambrose appeals to the appointment of the six cities of refuge as teaching us the need of such withdrawal; and, it must be added, entirely fails to make out his point. The cities where the accidental homicide was to be sheltered from the avenger of blood cannot be made to tell us anything about the duty of being unworldly. With more propriety does he allege the advice of the parents of Jacob, that he should flee from his brother to Padan-aram; though even here one fails to see how Jacob in Laban's house, though certainly in retirement from his home, could be considered as an instance of shrinking from the world. Nor does St. Paul, let down in a basket from the window in Damascus, and flying from Aretas, teach us, as Ambrose says, a lesson of *flight* from the world's intemperance and impurity. The ejaculation of David, *O that I had wings like a dove*, has reference rather to escape from enemies than from worldliness; and can only by a certain violence be made to apply, as Ambrose makes it apply, to the subject of his discourse. Elijah, Elisha, St. John the Baptist, Lot in his retreat from Sodom, and Susanna in her privacy, are far more to the purpose; he quotes them, but unfortunately does not dwell on them. On the whole, this

book ; though eminently devout, and not inelegant in
its language, is the poorest and weakest of the saint's
writings.

JACOB AND THE BLESSED LIFE.   These two books
are also of the year 387.   In the first, Ambrose shows
that the life of virtue is the truly blessed life : it is
attained by self-restraint on the part of men, wisdom,
and discipline, aided and fostered by the grace of
Christ.   To Him we must cling, whatever may betide
us ; for outward troubles do not interfere with the
blessed life in Him.

In the second book we are shown how Jacob (and
others), though under trial, enjoyed this blessed life.
This is brought out in a comment, partly moral,
chiefly mystical, on the various points in the life of
Jacob.   Esau, we learn, represents the Synagogue,
Jacob the Church ; the goodly raiment of Esau given
to Jacob is the privileges forfeited by the Jews and
given to the Church.   The singular device of the rods
in the sheepfold is a preaching of the Trinity ; for
the green poplar, hazel, and chestnut are in the LXX.
storax, walnut, and plane ; and of these storax, which
yields incense, signifies the Father, to whom incense is
offered ; walnut, of which Aaron's rod was made (so the
LXX. has it, instead of "almond"), betokens the priesthood of the Son ; and the plane-tree, on which vines are
trained (though Horace says the reverse), is the symbol
of the Holy Spirit.   After Jacob's departure, Laban,
whose name means "white," for *Satan is transformed
into an angel of light*, demands his property of Jacob,
and receives nothing, for *the prince of this world
cometh, and hath nothing in Me.*   Here Jacob is a

type not of the Church, but of Christ ; and so he is
in the interpretation of his marriage. Leah, the
tender-eyed, is the purblind Law, Rachel the Church
of the Gospel. Both belong to the Lord ; but He
loved Rachel first and best. Lastly, Jacob is the
likeness of the human soul : the wrestling with God
is striving to become like Him, the touch of the
thigh means the imparting the knowledge of Christ
crucified, and so, as *he halted upon his thigh, the sun
rose upon him*, that is, Divine illumination came by
the teaching of the cross.

Blessed thus in his life, the patriarch was also
blessed in his death, when he uttered the prophetic
benedictions : so, too, was Joseph in prison, Isaiah
in martyrdom, Jeremiah in the dungeon, Daniel in
the lions' den, and the mother of the Maccabees,
when she and her sons suffered for the truth's sake.
This last allusion sends the author off into an account
of the suffering of ths Maccabees, with a warm panegyric on their firmness under the cruel persecution of
the tyrant Antiochus, with which the book concludes.

The discourses on JOSEPH and the BLESSINGS OF
THE PATRIARCHS, delivered later on in the year 387,
and collected into two books, are, like the second on
Jacob, almost entirely mystical. In the former
Joseph is set before us as a type of Christ, and the
events of his life are shown to be figures of something connected with the Saviour. His sheaf adored
by the sheaves, and himself by the sun, moon, and
stars, tell of the Deity of Christ, and his father's
rebuke of the blindness of the Jews, who rejected
their Lord. He is sent to seek his brethren, is hated

by them, they seek to slay him, and finally hand him over to the heathen : just so it was with Christ. The coat stripped off him is the flesh of Christ, and this alone was torn and stained with blood; the Deity of Christ could not suffer. Brought down into Egypt, Joseph was a type of the Lord, who came down to sinful men.

Here the stream of Evangelical interpretation is interrupted. We expect to hear how Joseph in his temptation was a figure of our Lord in His, and how in descending into the prison and in coming out of it he foreshowed the burial and resurrection of Jesus. But we find none of this.; only a tirade against women and courtiers. Evidently Ambrose had not forgotten his disputes with Justina and the usher Calligonus.

From the advance of Joseph to dignity the thread is taken up again. His ring, and vesture, and chariot, signify the priesthood, wisdom, and dignity of Jesus; his Egyptian wife is the figure of the Gentile Church; the resort of all to him for food shows how all must come to Jesus for the food of their souls. And so his brethren came to him without Benjamin at first, as the Apostles came to Christ without St. Paul, of whom Benjamin is the representative; as Benjamin was kept in his old home, so St. Paul was kept from Christ by the Law. But at last Benjamin is permitted to go, and Reuben the Law, and Judah the Gospel, are sureties for him. The cup in the sack is the special gifts which St. Paul enjoyed : " He gives not all things to all men. Corn is given to many, the cup to one. . . . It is not every one, but the prophet only, who says, *I will receive the cup of salvation, and call on the name of the Lord.*" Then Joseph causes all men to go out from before him, for Christ was sent to the house of Israel only, and then embraces Benjamin, as Christ revealed Himself to St. Paul, and embraced him with the arms of His mercy. Pharaoh is glad, that is, the Gentile Church rejoices over the redemption of the Jews ; and finally, Jacob is brought by his sons from starving Canaan to Joseph and abundance, even as God's people are brought from the trammels of the Law into the abundant grace of the Church of Christ.

The history of Joseph is naturally followed by the BLESSINGS OF THE PATRIARCHS, an exposition almost exclusively Messianic of the benedictions in chapter xlix. of Genesis. As Ambrose renders from the LXX. version, his text differs largely from the Vulgate, Latin, and from ours. The blessing, or rather censure, of Reuben does not, as the Jews erroneously imagine, refer to the sin he had committed ; the reference is not to the past, but to the future. It foretells the insults and death of Christ ; and the "couch" is the Cross, on which saints rest, but which was "defiled" when Christ's body was nailed on it by the Jews. Similarly the censure of Simeon and Levi is prophetic. It does not refer to their dealings with the Shechemites, which were excusable if not praiseworthy, or Moses would not have uttered a blessing on Levi, to be fulfilled in the fact that our Lord was connected with that tribe, as we gather from the priestly names Levi and Nathan in His genealogy as given by St. Luke. It was fulfilled

when the priests and scribes took counsel against
Jesus and put Him to death, for Simeon was the
tribe of scribes, and Levi that of priests.   Judah, the
lion's whelp, betokens the Son of God. *From the
prey* is rendered by the LXX. and Ambrose, "from
the rod," an expression which is referred to the *rod
out of the stem of Jesse. He stooped down, who shall
raise him up?* foretells the burial of Christ, and His
resurrection through His own power, not another's.
Shilo is rendered in LXX. (according to the reading
which Ambrose adopts), "he for whom it is reserved"; and this is interpreted of Christ, for Whom
the Church is gathered together and reserved.   The
ass bound to the vine represents the Gentile Church
bound to the True Vine ; the garments are the
Manhood *washed in wine*, that is, filled with the
spirit and purified, and the *clothes washed in the blood
of grapes*, are the nations cleansed by the blood of
Him who hung like a grape on the cross.   The *eyes*
glad (A.V. *red*) with wine, are prophets who see
visions by the Spirit ; the *teeth* whiter than (A.V. *white
with*) *milk*, are Apostles, who, cleansed and whitened
by grace, feed first themselves and then others on
milk as a preparation for stronger food ; as it is said,
*I have fed you with milk and not with meat, for
hitherto ye were not able to bear it.*   Zabulon is the
Church, a haven from the storms of heresy, and the
sea of unbelief ; *and his border shall be unto Zidon*,
that is, she receives sinners and Gentiles.   Issachar
"desired the good, resting between the lots"; such
is the LXX. rendering of the *strong ass crouching
down between two burdens*, and prefigures Him Who

chose the good, and rested between the Old and New Testaments. *He saw the land*, that is, the nations of the earth, *that it was pleasant*, for by grace they should bring forth good works in abundance ; and *He bowed His shoulder to bear* the cross and the sins of men.   Dan is antichrist, the judge and the tyrant.   But he will not prevail over God's chosen ; the serpent bit the heel of Christ, so that He fell ; but He fell not on His face, He fell backward, and so still looked up to God; and even thus His people will still wait for the Lord's salvation.   In his version of the blessing of Gad, Ambrose's Greek halts.   The word we render "troop" is in the LXX. "a pirate-crew," correctly enough.   Misled by a similarity of words, Ambrose translates the passage "temptation tempted him, and he himself tempted them forthwith"; and understands it of the treacherous questions asked of Christ, and the questions which He put in reply.   Asher is of course the *Bread of Life*, and the *royal dainties* he yields are the Holy Eucharist.   The Hebrew word for "hind" also means "the bough of an oak"; and the blessing of Naphthali in the LXX. runs "a bough at liberty, yielding beauty in its produce." Ambrose makes it "a vine."   In the discourses on Jacob, the vine is Christ; here he considers the "vine at liberty" to be the people of God, a branch of the True Vine, showing growth in grace.   Joseph, both in the sermons on Jacob and in these, is a type of Christ.   The *fruitful bough* is with Ambrose "son to be ennobled," and *over the wall*, "return to me," referring plainly, he says, to Christ's ascension and return to the Father; the blessings prevailing *unto*

N

the utmost bound of the everlasting hills are His head-
ship over all.

Benjamin, as in the previous book, is a type of
St. Paul. He (in Ambrose's version) "shall eat still
in the morning, and towards evening distribute meat
to princes"; for St. Paul was a wolf when he perse-
cuted, but as Apostle of the Gentiles distributed
spiritual food to princes, as to Sergius Paulus and
Publius of Malta.

The DEFENCE OF THE PROPHET DAVID (384) is
another set of Scriptural expositions. They were delivered to meet the difficulty felt and expressed by some
in seeing a man of God in an adulterer and murderer.
Ambrose explains that God allows His saints to
show weakness, in order that they, as St. Paul says,
may not be *exalted above measure*, and that we, seeing
them to be of like infirmity with ourselves, may not
think it hopeless to imitate them. David, however,
is to be highly commended, because with all the
temptations of rank and power surrounding him, he
only fell once. The goodness of his character is
seen in his treatment of Saul, Absalom, Shimei; in
his choice of the punishment for his pride in num-
bering the people; in his refusal of the water of
the well of Bethlehem,—though therein is a mystery,
for he really wanted not material water, but the
precious blood of Jesus, who was born at Bethlehem.
After this exordium begins a short "Enarration" on
the fifty-first Psalm, the expression of David's penitence; and, as such, his own defence of himself. It
has much evangelic teaching in it: *Wash me*, speaks
to the Christian of holy baptism; *I acknowledge my*

transgressions, of Christian penitence ; *Thou shalt open my lips*, of forgiveness; *the sacrifices of righteousness*, of the sacrifice of Jesus Christ.

The COMPLAINT OF JOB AND DAVID might be entitled, On the Misery of Man. The discourses comprised in these four books belong most likely to the sad year 383, when famine and sword afflicted the Empire, and Church and State alike were thrown into mourning by the death of Gratian. Ambrose shows, in a running comment on portions of the book of Job and of the Psalter, how each in his own way bewails the wretchedness of men ; Job sternly and vehemently, David more gently, as befits the hart panting after the waterbrooks, the type of Christ. Job laments our weakness and ignorance, our continual trials and temptations, the fears that beset us. David in the Psalms speaks of sorrow and tears, and complains how God appears to forsake us, and the righteous seems to be confounded with the wicked. Both unite in surprise at the prosperity of the ungodly. The true consolation is to be found in thoughts of the providence of God, and in the possession of Christ. The ungodly may prosper for the present, but they lose their future.

The discourses on TOBIAS (377), ELIJAH AND FAST-ING (390), AND NABOTH THE JEZREELITE (395), pertain rather to the pastor than the theologian. They are neither expositions of Scripture nor statements of doctrine, but strong protests against the common and fashionable vices of the day. Those on Tobias are among Ambrose's earlier sermons. They are directed against the money-lender. This personage

has always been a difficulty; he is a trouble to us
now in India, and indeed is known and dreaded all
over the East, while the West is far from being insensible of his presence. Nor was he less of a
trouble in earlier times, and among the Romans.
The Twelve Tables in B.C. 450 tried to meet the
evil by fixing the legal maximum rate of interest at
unciarium fenus, one-twelfth of the capital per year of
ten months, or, as we should express it, 10 per cent.
per annum. The Lex Genucia in 341 prohibited
the taking of interest entirely; but it was impossible
to enforce the law, and the maximum legal rate was
eventually fixed at *centesimæ*, or 12 per cent., which
arrangement continued till the time of Justinian,
who altered the rate to 6 per cent. But extortionate
and illegal demands were not rare : Tacitus sighs
over the evil of usury, and Horace alludes to 60
per cent. paid in advance. In the Christian Church
there always was a feeling against lending money on
interest, and Ambrose denounces it. It has been
imagined that he did not object to all interest, but
only to an illegal and enormous rate ; but he quotes
too distinctly the texts *hath not given his money upon
usury*, and *lends, hoping for nothing again*, to allow us
to think that he would tolerate usury even in the
most modest form. What he would have permitted
in our days, with our national debts and our regular
systems of banking and credit, is another question.
The fair dealing of Tobit, who demanded no interest
from Gabael on the money deposited with him, and
almost apologized for asking for the principal, sup-
plies the preacher with a text for a bitter invective

against the evil of money-lending. He points his
discourse here and there with a play on words;
fenus, interest, is compared with *fœnum*, hay, and
aleo, the dicer, with *leo*, the lion; and he does not
hesitate to compare the usurer with Judas and the
devil. We have a graphic description of the tricks
practised by the man of money in order to get the
prey into his claws. "I shall have to break up my
family plate to accommodate you; it will be a great
loss to me; what amount of interest will compensate
for the loss of the workmanship? But I will do it
for *you* as a friend, and when you pay me I can have
the plate re-made. Let me have the interest on the
1st of the month regularly, and I will not press for
the principal, if you cannot make it up." Then we
have the swarm of harpies that crowd about the man
who has borrowed money; it soon runs away, for
the perfumer, and spice-dealer, and poulterer, and
fishmonger, and wine-merchant, are all at him; he
lives splendidly, till at last the money-lender makes
his call, and then he is in sad trouble; he sells his
fine clothes and his wife her jewels for half their
value, to pay the interest only. Again, we are shown
the usurer at the side of a young man of fortune, just
come into his property: "a capital estate for sale,
an admirable investment—I can find the purchase-
money, and it is at your service." The interest is
allowed to accumulate, and is added to the principal,
till the debtor is at the creditor's mercy, and passes
his days and nights in misery, trembling at every
knock. And so at last children have been sold to
pay their father's debts, and the rites of burial have

been refused to persons who died unable to pay. In one of these cases, Ambrose tells us, he ordered the funeral procession to go and stop in the front of the creditor's house till he was shamed into giving way. Then the money-lender watches gamblers, incites them to continue their play, and volunteers to lend money when needed; and thus even Huns, though subject to no one else, have been obliged to succumb to him. The borrower, however, is not without blame; he should not accept a loan if he has no prospect of being able to pay; and it is absurd to swallow the bait when the hook is so plainly to be seen; even a fish would not be so foolish. It may be objected, why does the bishop go out of his way to attack an old-established custom? this money-lending and usury-taking is no new fashion. "No more is sin," is the reply, "it is the oldest of fashions; but this is no plea in its favour." On the whole, we had better follow the example of Tobit: the only usury that is not wrong is spiritual profit; the best interest is to be looked for hereafter, not here.

The sermons on ELIJAH AND FASTING deal with the luxury, and especially the drunkenness, of the day. Ambrose is an ascetic, and a strict temperance man; he admits, however, the lawfulness of a moderate use of wine. "God knew," he says, speaking of the vine in the Hexaëmeron, "that wine temperately drunk procured health and increased discretion, . . . but when immoderately taken was the cause of crime. . . . Abundance of corn, wine, and oil given us by the Lord from the dew of heaven is

reckoned. among the choicest blessings." And, in
the *Abraham*, "so drink as not to be overtaken."
But the picture that he draws in these discourses of
the habits of his day with regard to intoxicating
liquor is very darkly shaded. We feel a sort of grim
comfort in learning that things are no worse in this
respect now among ourselves than they were at Milan
fifteen centuries ago. He describes men without a
shirt to their backs, or a halfpenny to pay for the
day's expenses, let alone the next day's, sitting in
front of the taverns, and chattering grandly on politics, or what not, with an occasional fight, while they
drink out a week's earnings; he takes us to the
officers' mess, where, decked out with their gilded
belts, Babylonian sashes, and golden gorgets, and
with a grand display of plate on the table, they drink
before dinner, drink at dinner, and after dinner drink
heavily against one another—in all such parties to
refuse to drink the Emperor's health is considered a
mark of disaffection. At last, after bragging loudly
of their martial exploits, they are hoisted up on their
horses by their grinning attendants, only to roll off
again, or fall dead drunk on the floor, and are carried
home on their shields. Others have a way of
swilling large bumpers at a draught; to take breath
is an offence, and the offender must pay forfeit. Nor
is the evil confined to men; women may be seen in
the streets behaving indecorously under the influence
of liquor, to the amusement of dissipated young men
and their own deep disgrace. The results are profli-
gacy, disease, insanity—the preacher describes, indeed, some of the symptoms of *delirium tremens*—and

poverty also; but for intemperance there would be no slavery. Gluttony and luxurious living, too, are despicable; one does not like to think of the alter-cations between the master and his cook about the price of fish, foie gras, and pheasants, and the hard work, and hard beatings besides, in the kitchen which attend upon a great dinner.

Denunciations of luxurious living, and the extravagance which is its companion, are not confined to these discourses. We hear in the *Cain and Abel* of the saloon with its sculptured walls, of the marble floor covered with slopped perfumes and spilt wine, with fish-bones and faded flowers; of the laughter, plaudits, and general din of the guests: in the *Tobias* of the absinthe bitters and the rare desserts: in the *Hexaëmeron* of fowls stuffed with oysters, gilded chandeliers, carefully-tended warming apparatus, ivory couches, droves of slaves: in the *Naboth* of the money frittered away on silk and jewels: in the *notes on St. Luke* (vii. 25) of the effeminate gentlemen who must needs dress in silk, because woollen was so heavy.

Fasting and sobriety, he proceeds to say, are best for the health both of soul and body; no one ever hurt himself by fasting. The first law given to man, *Thou shalt not eat of it*, recommended fasting (Ambrose says nothing of the *freely eat* of the previous verse), and its violation was man's ruin. Abstinence is recommended to us in many ways. Animals set us an example; the very elephants do not drink too much; they do occasionally imbibe immense quantities of water, but this is only to discharge it from

their trunks on some offending tradesman.[1]   Noah's
one offence of drunkenness was committed in ignorance, and is a warning to us ; Lot and Haman warn
us also ; and Abraham, Moses, Elijah, Elisha, Daniel,
Judith, John the Baptist, tell us of the spiritual
blessings of temperance.

The sermons finish in a manner we are scarcely
prepared for.   The preacher launches out into a
denunciation of commerce, as ministering to luxury.
" God made the sea, not to be sailed upon, but
because of the beauty of the element. . . . It is tossed
with storms, you ought therefore to dread it, not to
use it."   He ends with an earnest exhortation to the
unbaptized no longer to delay their reception of the
Sacrament.

NABOTH THE JEZREELITE is the title of Ambrose's
last sermons, for the discourses on the 44th Psalm
were left unfinished.   They contain an eloquent and
withering denunciation of the rich who neglect the
poor.   Some squander their money on self-indulgence,
dress, and wine, and dainties.   Others are misers, so
stingy that one of them, when served with an egg,
complained bitterly that a fowl had been killed.
These heap up their corn year after year till their very
barns are bursting with the food kept back from sale
till the price is higher.   Meanwhile the poor, even
those engaged in ministering to luxury, are starving.
One, after many agonies, sells his children for bread,
and struggles with himself which he shall let go first ;

---

[1] It is amusing to find this traditional Indian story of the
elephant's revenge as early as the fourth century.

another prefers suicide to perishing with hunger; and only hesitates which mode of death he shall prefer. And the unfeeling rich come to church all the while, and fast too, but for their own advantage only, without a thought of their poorer brethren. This is not the true way of storing or of being rich. "If thou wilt be rich, be poor unto the world, that thou mayest be rich unto God. He that is rich in faith, in simplicity, in mercy, in wisdom, in knowledge, he is rich unto God. There are those who in poverty have abundance, and those who in the midst of riches are in want. The poor have abundance, whose *deep poverty abounded unto the riches of their liberality:* rich men have lacked and hungered." And again, "*I have no room where to bestow my fruits.* You have the means of making room, never fear. I take you at your own word. You have *much goods laid up for many years*, you may have abundance both for yourself and for others. You enjoy the general good harvest, why *pull down your barns ?* I will show you where you may better bestow your corn, where you may fence it in well, so that thieves may not be able to take it away. Enclose it in the heart of the poor, where no weevil can devour it, no lapse of time damage it. You have garners, the laps of the poor : you have garners, the houses of widows : you have garners, the mouths of infants, so that it may be said to you, *out of the mouths of babes and sucklings thou hast perfected praise.* These are garners which last for ever, these are barns which no future plenty can require you to pull down. . . . Be a spiritual hus-

bandman : sow what will bring you gain. It is good
to sow in widows' hearts. If the earth renders you
fruits more plentiful than it received, how much more
will the recompense of mercy render to you many
times what you have bestowed ! "

CHAPTER XIX.

AMBROSE AS A PASTOR.

THE influence which Ambrose seems from the first to have acquired and exercised over all that came in contact with him would show him, had we no other proof of it, to have been no ordinary man. It was not because he was a safe man for a judicious compromise, but because of his sterling and recognised value, that he was elevated from the magistrate's bench to the episcopate by the well-nigh unanimous voice of a diocese. He must have been singularly gentle and courteous, for both the Valentinians, Gratian, and Theodosius, loved him ; but there must have been something about him beyond mere gentleness and courtesy, for Valens and Justina were afraid of him, while they hated him, and all his comprovincial bishops and brother metropolitans looked up to and respected him, even if they did not entirely agree with him. The great Augustine, we know, venerated him. The Persian nobles who visited him at the time of the penitence of Theodosius were full of admiration when they left him. Whether the mosaic said to represent him is a real likeness or not is uncertain, but it shows just that mixture of firmness and gentleness which we should expect in the features of the young Consular elevated by his own great merits, and the grand Bishop, the master-mind in his own day of the Western Church. And we read much about him to the same effect. He was firm enough with Palladius and Auxentius : he had, as we have seen, the moral courage to break up the Church plate in order to raise money for the ransom of captives taken in the civil wars,[1] and to brave all the Arians' comments on the proceeding, with all their ferocious obloquy ; but still, as we have also seen, his biographer tells us " he was one of those who *rejoice with them that do rejoice, and weep with them that weep.*" The secrets of confidential intercourse do not seem in those days to have been very closely guarded, for we are further told " he uttered to none the causes of the offences which any one confessed to him, save only to God, with Whom he interceded, leaving a good example to priests who should come after him, that they should be intercessors with God, rather than accusers before men." And yet we fail to trace the same character in those of his letters which have come down to us. They are kindly, but stiff in the extreme. They are principally concerned with Scripture and theology ; the expositions they contain are mostly of the mystical kind, often very far-fetched. The coldness remarkable in his poetry shows itself in his correspondence. He writes to his sister, and always with the coldest respect, styling her " your holiness "; he condoles with Faustinus on the death of his sister in a frigid imitation of Sulpicius's letter to Cicero on the death of Tullia ; he encourages some clergy who

---

[1] *See* page 68.

had got disheartened under difficulties and were thinking of throwing up their orders; gives Vigilius advice on his consecration; expresses his profound respect for Simplician, and discusses some theological questions for him; and thanks Felix, bishop of Como, for a present of some remarkably fine truffles, all in the same correct but chilly strain.

The three books ON THE DUTIES OF MINISTERS (391) may be considered as a pastoral work, although they are by no means intended for the ministers of the Church alone. They contain a system of Christian ethics, framed, Ambrose himself tells us, on the model of Cicero's well-known three books, "On Duties," and addressed to his sons in the faith, just as Cicero's work was addressed to Marcus, his son. Duties, says Cicero, are concerned with virtue (honestum) and utility (utile). The first book must therefore discuss virtue, the second utility, and the third must compare the two together, and different degrees of the two with one another. The Christian pastor and moralist follows on the same lines, but he introduces a new element, unknown to, or disregarded by, Panætius and his Roman disciple—the future life. All good, and all utility, must be ultimately measured by reference to God and eternity. After a preface, somewhat in the Ciceronian style, he proceeds to discuss, in the first book, the virtues of mercy and compassion, modesty, decorum, freedom from anger, moderation; and after a somewhat digressive examination of these, during which he diverges to the subjects of Divine Providence, omniscience, and justice, and to the right way of managing the voice and gestures, of conversing, preaching, and arguing, he proceeds to a more set treatment of four heads of the virtuous. These he specifies as—1. Wisdom or prudence, the origin of the other three ; 2. Justice, the safeguard to society, to be combined with benevolence, both active and passive ; 3. Courage, both passive, in the form of calmness and endurance, and active, in the form of warlike bravery, as exhibited in the Maccabees ; 4. Self-restraint, or temperance.

In the discussion are inserted some hints to Levites, who hold the " *ministerium* " (deacons), and to those who have received " *sacerdotium*," or priesthood, a term which includes the presbyterate and episcopate. They are to take care and not to go to too many convivial parties, lest they have to listen to, and perhaps join in, something objectionable ; they are not to make too many jokes, nor to modulate their voices like actors ; the young deacons are never to visit ladies except in the company of a priest or bishop. The marriage of clergy is not highly approved, but is permitted, for Ambrose complains that whereas sons generally elected their father's profession in secular callings, especially the military, the sons of clergy rarely took to the ministry. But it is distinctly laid down that a second marriage is unlawful to a cleric, and is a bar to holy orders, even if contracted before baptism.

In the second book Ambrose, like Cicero, treats of the useful, or to use another word, of happiness. This consists in knowledge of God and freedom from sin, quite irrespective of external circumstances of abundance or need ; for many things which are held to be good are really hindrances to the Christian. Thus utility coincides with virtue; and the conditions of utility are love and confidence. For inspiring the latter we need wisdom and justice; love is promoted by a judicious liberality shown in acts of kindness, such as redeeming prisoners, and giving dowries to poor orphan girls. But liberality must not be injudicious. Here we have some hints which would almost suit almsgivers and charity-organizers among ourselves. " A sober measure must be observed, especially by priests, so as to dispense not in proportion to the loudness of the appeal, but the justice of the case; for in no other business is there such greediness in asking. Sturdy fellows, who have no plea but their vagabondism, come and expect to run away with all the money intended for the relief of the poor; and they are not satisfied with a trifle; they ask for more, making their clothes an argument in favour of their request, or trying to get their receipts increased by some pretence about their birthday. . . . Many pretend they are in debt; the truth should be looked into. Others complain that they have been sufferers by robbery; the injury must be proved, or their person known, that they may be relieved more freely." Remember that Joseph did not give away corn, he sold it, and did far more good by adopting that course. To these hints are added, as in the previous book, some pieces of advice to clergy. They should value good society; if they seek ecclesiastical honours, they should do so in the right way, not by favouring the rich, but by showing kindness to the poor; and, above all things, they should avoid avarice; they should keep their churches in good order, and be liberal to all. One of their great duties is to preserve intact the deposits of widows, after the example of the Bishop of Pavia. This prelate had in his custody some money belonging to a widow, which was claimed under an imperial warrant. By Ambrose's advice, he absolutely refused to give it up; and so stoutly did he defend the deposit that he at last got his own way, and saved the old lady's property.

The third book declares comparison between virtue and utility to be impossible, because in Christian morals, as has been before laid down, the good and the useful are the same. The rule where duties appear to conflict is not to seek one's own. If the question be put, as it is by Cicero from Hecato, whether in a shipwreck a drowning wise man may take away a plank from a fool, the answer is (like Hecato's), certainly not; we must think of others, not of ourselves. Following his model, Ambrose in this book cites a number of cases of adherence to, or violation of, duty. Some of them are classical, as that of the faithful friends Damon and Pytheas, the Pythagoreans, and the way in which Pythius the Sicilian swindled Canius in the sale of an estate, as told by Cicero himself. Some of them are Scriptural or apocryphal; and it is curious to find the singular tale of the sacred fire hidden by the priests at the Captivity, and recovered by Nehemiah (the priest, Ambrose calls him), as related in the 2nd book of Maccabees, alleged as an instance of fidelity, and also as containing a type of holy baptism. Again we have advice to the clergy.

They must not think too much of gain; they must not hunt for legacies, nor mix themselves up with lawsuits about money; and vows which cannot be fulfilled without doing wrong, like Herod's and Jephthah's, are not to be adhered to. (We may remark that Ambrose is of opinion that Jephthah's daughter was actually put to death.) And, to conclude, in dealing with our friends we must be frank with them, ready to bear much for them and from them, for friendship is a holy thing; but we must not do wrong for a friend's sake, any more than for our own.

The two books ON PENITENCE, assigned to the year 384, may, though partly of a theological character, most correctly be placed under the head of pastoral writings. The first book is almost entirely devoted to combating the error of the Novatians, the Plymouth Brethren of the 3rd and 4th centuries, who denied the Church's power of granting absolution, and refused communion to all who had been guilty of post-baptismal sin. Their founder, Novatian, opposed the election of Cornelius as successor to Fabian, Bishop of Rome, in 250, on the ground of inclination to undue laxity of discipline; and his followers got (Eusebius says, took) the name of Kathari, or Puritans. But we meet with hints that Novatian's character was not irreproachable; his rival, Cornelius, describes him as an unprincipled fellow; and Ambrose says his schism was not the result of offended purity so much as of mortification at not being himself elected bishop. The sect, as is usual with sects, split into two parties one allowing

absolution to lesser sins, the other, with Novatian
himself, rejecting it entirely. Though it does not
clearly appear that the Novatians limited in set terms
the mercy of God, and affirmed the necessary perdi-
tion of all who sinned after baptism, yet they seem
to have expressed themselves as if there were but
little hope for the guilty. "Those whom Christ
intercedes for, Novatian accuses. Those whom
Christ has redeemed unto salvation, Novatian con-
demns unto death. To those to whom Christ says,
*Take My yoke upon you, and learn of Me, for I am
meek*, Novatian says, 'I am ruthless.' On those to
whom Christ says, *Ye shall find rest unto your souls,
for My yoke is easy and My burden is light*, Novatian
lays a heavy burden, and a hard yoke." Ambrose
shows that their opinion is opposed to all the passages of Scripture which speak of God's mercy and
Christ's death for man. They argued, as extreme
Calvinists now argue, that to adopt any opinion but
theirs was to make God changeable; to which he
replies that God has declared to us that He is merciful; *for the Lord will not cast off for ever.* Their
objection that man cannot be the instrument of forgiveness, an objection against absolution not altogether unknown in our own day, is simply answered
by pointing out that, according to their own practice,
baptism, which conveyed remission of sin, and the
laying of hands on the sick, which brought bodily
health, were ministered by men. "To deliver to
Satan," an expression of St. Paul, does not mean, as
the Novatians seemed to think, the abandonment of
sinners, but their chastisement by the operation of

the evil one, as Job was by God's permission troubled and afflicted by him. And the same Apostle contrasts the binding and loosing powers of the Church in his question, *Shall I come unto you with a rod, or in love and in the spirit of meekness?* The rod is excommunication, the spirit of meekness is restitution to the sacraments, with a reference, probably, to the saving spiritual effect of Christian discipline.

In the second book the subject is treated generally, and without express reference to Novatian error. The passage from the Epistle to the Hebrews, *It is impossible to renew them again unto repentance,* cannot be meant by St. Paul to overthrow his own teaching : he sent absolution to the excommunicated Corinthian on his penitence, and therefore cannot have denied the possibility of such forgiveness. The real meaning of the text is that baptism cannot be repeated. The only sin that cannot be forgiven is blasphemy against the Spirit, that is, heresy and schism and guilt obstinately persevered in. Even Simon Magus had a place of repentance proffered him ; even Judas Iscariot might have obtained pardon, if he had offered his penitence not to Jews, but to Christ. Then Ambrose earnestly exhorts sinners to penitence, and tears, and self-accusation, and avowal of their errors ; not forgetting, as we know was his wont, to identify himself with his penitents. "Call then," he says (he has been speaking of the raising of Lazarus), "Thy servant forth. Though bound with the chains of my sins, my feet tied, and my hands fastened, and already buried with dead thoughts and works, at Thy call I shall come forth free, and be found one of those that sit at meat at Thy feast, and Thy house shall be filled with precious ointment, if Thou keep him whom Thou hast deigned to redeem. For it will be said, See how he, not nurtured in the Church's bosom, not trained from boyhood, but hurried from the tribunal, snatched from the vanities of this world, made familiar with the chorister's hymn instead of the court-crier's voice, remains in the priesthood, not by his own goodness, but by the grace of Christ, and sits down with the guests at the heavenly table. Preserve, O Lord, that gift of Thine which Thou didst bestow on me even though I fled from it. For I knew I was not worthy to be called a bishop, because I had given myself to this world ; but by Thy grace I am what I am."

As a theologian Ambrose was, we have seen, strenuous and indefatigable in teaching and defending the Deity of the Son and the Spirit. As a pastor he was equally strenuous and equally indefatigable in urging Christians, and Christian maidens especially, to abstain from marriage. He has left no less than six books of discourses preached on the subject, eloquent, earnest, almost fanatical ; of the three degrees of chastity, wedlock as exemplified in Susanna, widowhood in Anna, virginity in the Blessed Virgin, he holds up the third as the only real and glorious virtue. Though he qualifies his words here and there with a faint admission that marriage is not unlawful, not a crime, and that he must not be held to dissuade marriage, he expresses himself so strongly on the evils of wedlock and the blessings of celibacy, that we are not at all surprised at being told that the girls of North Italy took the vows in troops, and that ladies actually locked up their daughters to prevent their going to hear him preach. There were at this time a number of monasteries for men, but few convents for women ; we read of one at Bologna, but there seems to have been none in Milan. Those who took the vow of perpetual virginity received consecration at the hand of the bishop, and put on a veil, called *maforte,* but continued to live at home. They were required to dress and live plainly, to spend much time in prayer and the recitation of the Psalter, and to avoid visiting and entertainments. So intense was Ambrose's admiration of this unmarried life in women, that he mentions with approval the case of St. Pelagia of Antioch, a girl of fifteen, who, with her mother and sisters, committed deliberate suicide rather than comply with the wishes of those who desired them to accept husbands ; and quotes with some satisfaction what we should consider an unfilial and unfeeling reply on the part of a young lady, who being asked at her consecration whether she thought her father, if he had been living, would have approved of her remaining unmarried, answered, " Perhaps he was removed by death in order that there might be no bar to my carrying out my wishes." " Very religious," observes Ambrose, " though not quite so affectionate."

He began his teaching on celibacy very early. The three books On Virgins, inscribed to his sister Marcellina, and one On Widows, belong to the year 377. " A priest of three years' standing," is the term he applies to himself ; " even my fig-tree," he says, " will bear fruit after three years."

The Discourses On Virgins, and the one book On Viginity (378), all take the same line: the unmarried is the angelic life; impurity brought down angels to earth (for so, we have already seen, Ambrose inter-prets Gen. vi. 2), and purity raises earthly maidens to heaven : the Song of Songs shows that women should be wedded to Christ only; and we have numberless examples of the beauty of virginity: St. Agnes, the virgin martyr of twelve in the tenth persecution, on whose festival the first of the sermons was preached; St. Thecla, the disciple of St. Paul, whom the lion refused to touch ; the maiden martyr of Antioch, preserved from disgrace by a Christian soldier who changed clothes with her, and had the honour of dying with her ; and above all, the ever-virgin mother of Jesus, the pattern of the virginal life. We cannot help remark-ing that with all the honour that is paid by Ambrose to the memory of St. Mary, he does not say a word about her assumption or her intercession : her very entrance into heaven is spoken of as an event to come.

The book on Widows was addressed to a widow lady, who after violent affliction at her bereavement was thinking of marrying again. Ambrose advises her to remain under a vow of widowhood, which he con-siders next in merit to absolute celibacy; not, he says, because second marriages are unlawful, but because they are inexpedient.

In the year 392 Ambrose consecrated, or, as the phrase went, instituted, a young lady named after him, Ambrosia, the granddaughter of his great friend Eusebius of Bologna. The sermon preached by the

bishop on the occasion was, with a few additions, sent
to Eusebius shortly after. It repeats the old argu-
ments, with some good advice as to the rule of life of
a consecrated virgin, and is especially to be noted as
containing a very distinct dogmatic assertion of the
perpetual virginity of the Blessed Virgin, in spite of
the caution of St. Basil, that it is a subject we had
better not meddle with.

In the next year (393) Ambrose, as we have already
seen, retired from Milan to Bologna on the approach
of Eugenius. At Bologna he became possessed of
some relics of the martyrs Agricola and Vitalis.
These he conveyed to Florence, and placed in a new
church which he was invited to consecrate in that
city. The church was built at the expense of a rich
widow, named Juliana. The consecration sermon
was preached by Ambrose himself. One is amused
to read that, having in the course of it spoken of the
foundress, by a slip of the tongue, as Judæa, instead
of Juliana, he dexterously turns his mistake to good
account: "My tongue made no mistake, but a defini-
tion, for *in Judæa (Jewry) is God known.*" The
sermon, or the book into which it has been developed,
is entitled " An Exhortation to Virginity." The
preacher begins by addressing both young men and
young women in the name of Juliana, and exhorting
them to give themselves to that celibate life to which
she had already dedicated not only her three daughters,
but also her son Laurentius, now a minister of the
church of her foundation ; and after seconding the
exhortation warmly in his own person, prays for a
blessing on the church and those who offered it and

themselves to God : " When Thou dost look upon that salutary offering, whereby the sin of this world is done away, look also on these offerings of holy chastity, and preserve them with Thy continual help, that they may become to Thee an odour of a sweet savour, offerings acceptable, pleasing to the Lord Christ, and that Thou mayest deign to keep their whole spirit, soul, and body blameless until the day of Thy Son, our Lord Jesus Christ."

THE WORKS OF ST. AMBROSE.

THE undoubtedly authentic writings of St. Ambrose are as follows, arranged as far as possible in chronological order :—

A.D.

375. Paradise. One book.
     Cain and Abel. Two books.
377. Virgins. Three books.
     Widows. One book.
     Tobias. One book.
378. Virginity. One book.
379. The Faith. Five books.
     Noah and the Ark. One book.
     On the Decease of his Brother Satyrus.
     Faith in the Resurrection. A Second Book
        on the Decease of Satyrus.
381. The Holy Spirit. Three books.
382. The Incarnation. One book.
383. The Complaint of Job and David. Four
        books.
384. Defence of the Prophet David. One book.
     Penitence. Two books.
386. Commentary on Ps. cxix.
     Commentary on St. Luke. Ten books.
387. Abraham. Two books.
     Isaac and the Soul. One book.
     The Benefit of Death. One book.
     The Mysteries. One book.
     Retreat from the World. One book.
     Jacob and the Blessed Life. One book.
     Joseph. One book.

387. The Blessings of the Patriarchs. One book.

389. Hexaëmeron, or the Six Days of Creation. Six books.

390. Commentary on Ps. i., xlvi., xlviii., xlix., lxii. Elijah and Fasting. One book.

391. The Duties of Ministers. Three books.

392. Speech of Consolation on the Death of Valentinian II.
The Institution of a Virgin. One book.

393. Exhortation to Virginity. One book.

394. Commentary on Ps. xxxvi.–xli.

395. Speech on the Death of Theodosius.
Naboth the Jezreelite. One book.

397. Commentary on Ps. xliv. (Left unfinished.)
Eighty-four Letters, from A.D. 379–A.D. 396.
Seven Public Letters, between A.D. 381 and A.D. 389.
Twelve Hymns.

Theodoret has preserved a Greek version of a fragment of a lost work, "An Exposition of the Faith"; and another lost work, "On the Sacrament of Regeneration, or on Philosophy, against Plato," is alluded to by St. Augustine in his "Retractations."[1] St. Ambrose himself speaks of a commentary of his own on Isaiah, which is often referred to by St. Augustine.

A second "Defence of David,"

[1] The occasion of the allusion is curious. Augustine stated in his work "On Christian Doctrine" that Ambrose said Plato learnt of Jeremiah in Egypt. In the Retractations Augustine admits he was wrong, and shows, from the work alluded to, that Ambrose was of a different opinion. The idea involves a gross anachronism, of course, as Augustine himself shows in his "City of God."

A Virgin's Fall, in one book,
The Sacraments, in six books,
are sometimes attributed to Ambrose, but most probably are not from his pen.

The following have also been attributed to him, but are undoubtedly spurious :—

The Fall of Jerusalem. Five books.
Commentary on St. Paul's Epistles.
Commentary on the Seven Visions in the Apocalypse.
The Forty-two Resting-places of the Children of Israel.
The Trinity.
The Orthodox Faith.
The Dignity of the Priesthood.
To a Consecrated Virgin.
Sixty-three Sermons.
Four Epistles.
Two Prayers before Mass.
The Holy Ghost.
Penitence.
Seventy Hymns.
The Two Genealogies of Christ.
The Dignity of Man's Condition.
An Exorcism.
The Acts of St. Sebastian.
The Conflict of Vices and Virtues.
The Calling of the Gentiles.
The Customs of the Brahmins.
Epistles of Certain Philosophers.
Two Letters about a Monk possessed with a devil.
Explanation of the Creed.
Letter to St. Jerome on the Faith.

CHRONOLOGY.

A.D.

325. Council of Nicæa.   Birth of St. Gregory Nazianzen.

326. St. Athanasius, at 28, made Bishop of Alexandria.

329. Birth of St. Basil.

331. Birth of St. Gregory Nyssen and St. Jerome.

335. Arian Synod at Tyre.   First exile of St. Athanasius.

336. Death of Arius.   Marcus Bishop of Rome, on the death of St. Silvester.

337. Death of Constantine the Great.   Julius I. Bishop of Rome.

338. St. Athanasius restored.

340. Constantine II. killed at Aquileia.   Death of Alexander, Bishop of Constantinople, who is succeeded by Paul. Death of Eusebius.   Birth of St. Ambrose.

341. Second exile of St. Athanasius.   7th Council of Antioch.

343. Photinus begins his heretical teaching.

347. Birth of St. Chrysostom.   Council of Sardica.   St. Athanasius restored.

348. Birth of Prudentius, the Christian poet.

349. Synod of Sirmium against Photinus.

350. Death of Constans.   St. Hilary Bishop of Poictiers. Magnentius proclaimed Emperor in the West.

351. Condemnation of Photinus by a semi-Arian Council. Macedonius Bishop of Constantinople.

352. Liberius Bishop of Rome.

353. St. Ambrose removes to Rome on his father's death. Death of Magnentius.

354. Birth of St. Augustine.   Death of the Cæsar Gallus. Marcellina receives the consecration of a sister from Liberius on Christmas-Day.

355. The Arian Synod of Milan banishes Liberius, Bishop of Rome, Dionysius of Milan, and Lucifer of Cagliari. Third exile of Athanasius.   Auxentius Bishop of Milan.

356. St. Hilary of Poictiers banished by Constantine.

357. Liberius (according to Arian accounts) subscribes the Arian creed and returns to Rome.

359. Synod of Ariminum, in which the Catholics are deceived into surrendering the term Consubstantial. Macedonius deposed from Constantinople, and replaced by Eudoxius.

361. Julian succeeds Constantine.

362. Fourth exile of St. Athanasius.

363. Julian killed in Persia, and succeeded by Jovian. St. Athanasius restored. Felix II. Bishop of Rome. Commencement of Luciferian schism.

364. Death of Jovian. Valentinian I. and Valens Emperors.

366. Damasus Bishop of Rome.

373. Death of St. Athanasius. Defeat of Firmus the Moor.

374. St. Ambrose, while holding the office of Consular of Liguria, is elected Bishop of Milan, baptized, and consecrated. St. Martin Bishop of Tours.

375. Death of Valentinian I. Gratian and Valentinian II. become Emperors.

376. Embassy of Ulfilas to Valens.

378. Battle of Adrianople : defeat and death of Valens. Death of St. Basil and of Ephraem Syrus. St. Gregory Nazianzen appointed Bishop of Constantinople.

379. Theodosius becomes Emperor : defeats the Goths. Death of Satyrus, brother of St. Ambrose.

380. Baptism of Theodosius. Priscillian condemned at the Council of Saragossa.

381. Council of Constantinople. Synod of Aquileia, and condemnation of Palladius and Secundianus. Law of Theodosius against the Arians. St. Gregory Nazianzen confirmed in the Bishopric of Constantinople : resigns, and Nectarius is appointed.

382. Synod at Rome.

383. Murder of Gratian : first embassy of St. Ambrose to Maximus.

384. St. Ambrose's dispute with Symmachus. St. Augustine comes to Milan. Siricius Bishop of Rome. Priscillian put to death.

385. Conversion of St. Augustine. St. Ambrose defends the Churches against Justina and the Arians.

386. Consecration of a new basilica at Milan. Death of St. Cyril of Jerusalem.

387. Baptism of St. Augustine. St. Ambrose's second embassy to Maximus. Flight of Justina and Valentinian.

388. Death of Justina. Defeat and death of Maximus. The riot at Antioch. St. Chrysostom's homily "On the Statues."

389. Theodosius and Valentinian at Milan. Condemnation of Jovinian.

390. Massacre at Thessalonica. Excommunication and penitence of Theodosius.

392. Murder of Valentinian II. Eugenius emperor. St. Ambrose retires to Florence.

394. Battle of the Frigidus : defeat and death of Eugenius and Arbogastes.

395. Death of Theodosius : Arcadius and Honorius emperors. Marriage of Arcadius and Eudoxia. St. Augustine Bishop of Hippo. The Huns invade the East. Death of Rufinus.

396. Message to St. Ambrose from Fritigil, Queen of the Marcomanni. Alaric the Goth escapes from Stilicho.

397. Death of St. Ambrose, on Easter Eve, April 4. He is succeeded by Simplician.

398. St. Chrysostom Bishop of Constantinople. Gildo the Moor, defeated by his own brother Mascezel, commits suicide.

399. Anastasius I. Bishop of Rome. Marriage of Honorius to Maria, daughter of Stilicho.

WYMAN AND SONS, PRINTERS,
GREAT QUEEN STREET, LINCOLN'S INN FIELDS,
LONDON, W.C.

PUBLICATIONS

OF THE

Society for Promoting Christian Knowledge.

•

ALONE WITH GOD; OR, HELPS TO THOUGHT AND
PRAYER. For the use of the Sick; based on short
passages of Scripture. By the Rev. F. BOURDILLON,
M.A., Author of "Lesser Lights." 12mo. *Cloth boards* 1 6

A MODE OF CATECHIZING. By the Rev. Temple
HILLYARD, Rector of Oakford, Devon, Canon of Chester
Cathedral. 18mo.............................*Cloth boards* 1 0

APOSTLES' CREED (THE). Aid to its Reception;
Duties under it: being a plain Exposition of the
Creed, with some Practical Observations. Eight
Lectures. By the Rev. C. J. D'OYLY. Fcap. 8vo.
Cloth boards 1 0

BIBLE PLACES; OR, THE TOPOGRAPHY OF THE
HOLY LAND. By the Rev. Canon TRISTRAM, Author
of "Land of Israel," "Scenes in the East," &c. A
new and revised edition. With Map and numerous
Woodcuts. Crown 8vo. *Cloth boards* 4 0

CHRISTIAN FATHERS (THE). Lives of Ignatius,
Polycarp, Justin, Irenæus, Cyprian, Athanasius,
Hilary, Basil, Gregory Nazianzen, Ambrose, Jerome,
Chrysostom, Augustine, Gregory the Great, Bede,
Bernard. By the Rev. G. G. PERRY, M.A., Preben-
dary of Lincoln, &c. ....*Cloth boards* 3 6

CHRISTIAN MISSIONS BEFORE THE REFORMATION.
By the Rev. F. F. WALROND, M.A., Vicar of Rusthall,
Kent. With four full-page Illustrations on toned
paper. Post 8vo. ....*Cloth boards* 2 6

14-6-79.]   [12mo.

CHRISTIANS UNDER THE CRESCENT IN ASIA. By the Rev. E. L. CUTTS, B.A., Author of "Turning Points of Church History," &c. With numerous Illustrations. Crown 8vo. .... *Cloth boards* 5 0

CHURCH HISTORY IN ENGLAND, from the Earliest Times to the Period of the Reformation. By the Rev. ARTHUR MARTINEAU, M.A. 12mo. *Cloth boards* 3 0

CHURCH HISTORY (SKETCHES OF), during the first Six Centuries. By the Rev. J. C. ROBERTSON, M.A. Part I. With Map. 12mo. ...... *Cloth boards* 1 0

———————————— **Part II., from** the Seventh Century to the Reformation. 12mo. *Cloth boards* 1 0

Parts I. and II. in a volume................. *Cloth boards* 2 0

COMFORTER (THE). By the Rev. W. R. CLARK, Vicar of Taunton. Fcap. 8vo. .... *Cloth boards* 2 0

GOSPELS (THE FOUR), arranged in the form of an English Harmony, from the Text of the Authorized Version. By the Rev. J. M. FULLER, M.A. With Analytical Table of Contents and 4 Maps ...*Cloth bds.* 1 6

HISTORY OF THE ENGLISH CHURCH. In short Biographical Sketches. By the Rev. JULIUS LLOYD, M.A., Author of "Sketches of Church History in Scotland." Post 8vo....................... *Cloth boards* 2 0

HISTORY OF THE JEWISH NATION (A), from the Earliest Times to the Present Day. By E. H. PALMER, Esq., M.A., Author of "The Desert of the Exodus," &c. With Map of Palestine and numerous Illustrations. Crown 8vo. .... *Cloth boards* 5 0

LAND OF ISRAEL (THE), a Journal of Travel in Palestine, undertaken with special reference to its Physical Character. By the Rev. Canon TRISTRAM, Third Edition Revised. With two Maps, and numerous Illustrations. Large post 8vo. ....*Cloth boards* 10 6

LESSER LIGHTS; or, Some of the Minor Cha- racters of Scripture traced, with a View to Instruction and Example in Daily Life. By the Rev. F. BOURDILLON, M.A. Post 8vo..............*Cloth boards* 2 6

LITANY (THE). With an Introduction, Explanation of Words and Phrases, together with Illustrative and Devotional Paraphrase. By the Rev. EDWARD JACOB BOYCE, M.A., Rector of Houghton, Hants. Fcap. 8vo........................ *Cloth boards* 1 0

NARRATIVE OF A MODERN PILGRIMAGE through Palestine on Horseback, and with Tents. By the Rev. ALFRED C. SMITH, M.A. Numerous Illustrations, and four Coloured Plates. Crown 8vo... *Cloth boards* 5 0

ON THE NATURE AND OFFICE OF GOD THE HOLY GHOST. By the Rev. S. C. AUSTEN, Vicar of Stokenchurch, Oxon, author of "The Divinity of our Blessed Lord." Fcap. 8vo...................*Cloth boards* 1 0

PALEY'S EVIDENCES. A New Edition, with Notes, Appendix, and Preface. By the Rev. E. A. LITTON. Post 8vo.............................*Cloth boards* 4 0

PALEY'S HORÆ PAULINÆ. A New Edition, with Notes, Appendix, and Preface. By the Rev. J. S. HOWSON, D.D., Dean of Chester. Post 8vo. *Cloth boards* 3 0

PRAYER-BOOK (HISTORY OF THE). By Miss PEARD, Author of "One Year." *Cloth boards* 1 0

READINGS ON THE FIRST LESSONS FOR SUNDAYS and Chief Holy Days, according to the New Table. By the Rev. PETER YOUNG, Author of "Daily Readings on the Life of our Lord." Crown 8vo. *In two volumes* 8 0

RELIGION FOR EVERY DAY. Lectures for Men. By ALFRED BARRY, D.D., D.C.L., Principal of King's College, London. Fcap. 8vo. ....*Cloth boards* 1 0

ST. CHRYSOSTOM'S PICTURE OF HIS AGE. Post 8vo...................................... *Cloth boards* 2 0

ST. CHRYSOSTOM'S PICTURE OF THE RELIGION OF HIS AGE. Post 8vo. .... *Cloth boards* 1 6

SCENES IN THE EAST. Consisting of Twelve Coloured Photographic Views of Places mentioned in the Bible, beautifully executed, with Descriptive Letterpress. By the Rev. Canon TRISTRAM, Author of "Bible Places," &c.... *Cloth, bevelled boards, gilt edges* 7 6

SERVANTS OF SCRIPTURE (THE). By the Rev. *s. d.*
JOHN W. BURGON, B.D., Dean of Chichester. Post 8vo.
Cloth boards 1 6

SINAI AND JERUSALEM; or, Scenes from Bible
Lands. Consisting of Coloured Photographic Views
of Places mentioned in the Bible, including a Pano-
ramic View of Jerusalem, with descriptive Letterpress. By the Rev. F. W. HOLLAND, M.A., Honorary
Secretary to the Palestine Exploration Fund. Demy
4to........................ *Cloth, bevelled boards, gilt edges* 7 6

SOME CHIEF TRUTHS OF RELIGION. By the
Rev. EDWARD L. CUTTS, B.A., Author of "St. Cedd's
Cross," "Turning Points of English and General
Church History," &c. Crown 8vo. ....*Cloth boards* 3 0

THE USE AND ABUSE OF THE WORLD. Sermons preached on the Sundays after Easter, 1873,
1874, 1875, in the Church of St. James, Piccadilly.
In Three Series. Post 8vo. *Cloth boards* ....*each* 1 6

The Three Series in One Volume .... *Cloth boards* 2 6

TURNING POINTS OF ENGLISH CHURCH HISTORY.
By the Rev. EDWARD L. CUTTS, B.A., Vicar of Holy
Trinity, Haverstock Hill, Author of "Some Chief
Truths of Religion." Crown 8vo..........*Cloth boards* 3 6

TURNING POINTS OF GENERAL CHURCH HISTORY.
By the Rev. E. L. CUTTS, B.A., Author of "Pastoral
Counsels," &c. Crown 8vo. .... *Cloth boards* 5 0

UNDER HIS BANNER. Papers on Missionary
Work of Modern Times. By the Rev. W. H. TUCKER.
With Map. Crown 8vo. New Edition...*Cloth boards* 5 0

VENTURES OF FAITH; OR, DEEDS OF CHRISTIAN
HEROES. By the Rev. J. J. HALCOMBE. With six
Illustrations on toned paper. Crown 8vo. *Cloth boards* 2 6

Depositories:

77, GREAT QUEEN STREET, LINCOLN'S INN-FIELDS, W.C.;

4, ROYAL EXCHANGE, E.C.; 48, PICCADILLY, W.; LONDON.

www.ingramcontent.com/pod-product-compliance
Lightning Source LLC
Chambersburg PA
CBHW030134030726
47498CB00007B/2696